BAD LUCK

BAD LUCK

pseudonymous bosch

Illustrations by Juan Manuel Moreno

LITTLE, BROWN AND COMPANY

New York Boston

Text copyright © 2016 by Pseudonymous Bosch
Interior illustrations copyright © 2016 by Juan C. Moreno
Spot art on pages 161, 162: © Happy Art/Shutterstock.com (dog icon),
LDDesign/Shutterstock.com (human icon), tulpahn/Shutterstock.com (fly and dragon icons)
Background art on pages 32, 33, 126, 127: © Martina Vaculikova/Shutterstock.com

Little, Brown and Company

Hachette Book Group
1290 Avenue of the Americas, New York, NY 10104
Visit us at lb-kids.com

Little, Brown and Company is a division of Hachette Book Group, Inc.
The Little, Brown name and logo are trademarks of Hachette Book Group, Inc.

The publisher is not responsible for websites (or their content) that are not owned by the publisher.

First Edition: February 2016

ISBN 978-0-316-32042-9

10 9 8 7 6 5 4 3 2 1

RRD-C

Printed in the United States of America

FOR RAPHAEL SIMON
(WHOSE NAME I KEEP FORGETTING)

...but it is one thing to read about dragons
and another to meet them.

—Ursula K. Le Guin, *A Wizard of Earthsea*

And might I add, it is one thing to meet dragons
and another to live to write about them.

—PB

BAMBOO
BAY

MOUNT
FORGE

LAVA
LAKE

PRICE
PUBLIC LIBRARY

OLD BARN

EGG
ROCK

THE RUINS

VOG

LAVA FIELDS

N
W E
S

CHAPTER
ONE

MUSTER

The *Imperial Conquest* had five swimming pools, four gyms, a three-story waterslide, a two-lane bowling alley, an outdoor movie theater, a giant climbing wall, a miniature golf course, an ice-cream parlor, a pizza parlor, a sushi bar, a taco stand, a twenty-four-hour arcade, an eighteen-and-under dance club, an eighteen-and-over casino (that was a little lax about its age limit), a full-service spa, and a multi-floor luxury shopping mall, but so far the thing Brett liked best about this gigantic cruise ship was the Jell-O parfait at the Lido Deck Snack Shack.

Jell-O and whipped cream. It was the perfect combination. Sweet and tangy. Rich and soft. He couldn't believe it had taken all twelve long years of his life to discover it.

Eating slowly to make his parfait last, Brett waded through the sea of sunbathers. He was the only person around who was fully clothed, not to mention wearing a bow tie—sometime in the sixth grade, Brett had decided that bow ties would be his "signature accessory"—and as usual he got some funny looks.

A sunburned boy pointed at him. "Hey, penguin, wrong cruise—North Pole is the other way."

"You mean South Pole," Brett replied automatically. "No penguins in the North. Just...elves."

And next time, try a higher SPF, he thought. Lobster.

A woman squinted at him from behind her sunglasses. "Are you my waiter? Where's my drink?"

"I don't know," said Brett. "Maybe you drank it?"

By the way, I'm not your waiter; my dad owns this ship, he almost added. But she probably wouldn't have believed him anyway.

Even though it happened to be true.

All he wanted to do was return to his stateroom and eat his parfait in peace. Was that too much to ask? Well, maybe just one more bite before he—

BEEP! BEEP! BEEP!

He almost choked when the alarm sounded. Three high-pitched beeps so loud they made his head hurt.

Brett looked down in dismay—a dribble of green Jell-O had landed on his bow tie. He could barely see over his chin, but he wiped it away as best he could.

"This is your captain speaking," said a woman over the ship's intercom. Her voice had a distinctive accent—Australian, it sounded to Brett. A good sign, he thought. (Australia was the home of the Great Barrier Reef, and if she could navigate the world's biggest coral reef, she could probably navigate anywhere.*) "Please report to your assigned muster room immediately. This is only a drill...."

Brett's muster room, the Shooting Stars Nightclub and Casino, was five floors down. As Brett entered, still clutching his parfait glass, a uniformed crew member stood onstage, trying to entertain everyone with a less-than-successful rendition of Michael Jackson's "Beat It."

The crowd booed happily.

"Oh, so you guys think you can do better, huh?" said the crew member, pretending to be insulted. "Well, our karaoke contest is tomorrow night, right after the magic show!"

He nodded to the poster behind him. It showed a big pair of bunny ears sticking out of a top hat:

---

* In fact, as I'm sure Brett would be the first to tell you, the Great Barrier Reef is not just one coral reef; it is a group of reefs that together make up the biggest structure in the world to have been built by living organisms—so big it can be seen from a spaceship. Or so they say. I myself have never seen it from a spaceship, only from a submarine—and once, memorably, from the mast of a catamaran.

NOW YOU SEE HIM...
NOW YOU DON'T!
An Evening of Magic and Mystery

Another crew member, whose badge read MIGUEL, PHILIPPINES, scanned Brett's cruise ID card, and Brett saw his own image flash across a small video screen, along with the words VIP—ALL ACCESS.

Miguel looked down at the husky, overdressed twelve-year-old in front of him. If he was suspicious of Brett's VIP status, he didn't say anything about it.

"I was wondering, Miguel," said Brett. "Why do they call this a muster room? Is it because you have to muster your courage when the ship is sinking?"

"Sorry, sir. I have no idea."

Miguel didn't look sorry. In fact, he looked irritated. Brett often had this effect on people. He wasn't sure why.

"Well, if I were you, I would look it up," Brett said helpfully. "Mustering is your job, after all."*

---

* ACTUALLY, THE REASON A MUSTER ROOM IS CALLED A MUSTER ROOM IS NOT SO MUSTERIOUS. *TO MUSTER* IS TO ASSEMBLE—AS IN TO ASSEMBLE TROOPS, OR IN THIS CASE TO ASSEMBLE PEOPLE ON A SHIP. SIMILARLY, *A MUSTER* IS A GATHERING OR AN ASSEMBLY OF PEOPLE, USUALLY IN THE MILITARY. THUS, *TO MUSTER ONE'S COURAGE* IS SIMPLY TO GATHER ONE'S COURAGE. *TO CUT THE MUSTARD*, MEANWHILE, MEANS TO SUCCEED OR

Before Brett could find a place to sit, Brett senior walked over with his smiling young fiancée, Amber, in tow.

"Junior! What took you so long?" he bellowed loudly enough to cause people to turn. "Good thing there isn't a real emergency!"

Brett cringed in embarrassment. It looked as though his father had come straight from the pool; he was wearing an open shirt and one of his just-a-little-too-small bathing suits. A gold chain hung from his neck, snagging on his hairy chest. At his side, the always-sunny Amber was dressed in sparkly yellow workout clothing. It seemed to Brett that she had an entire rainbow's worth of yoga pants. Both his father and Amber wore life vests around their necks.

"Where's your vest? Never mind—" Brett's father turned to Amber, who was busy applying strawberry lip balm to her already balmy lips. "Can you grab him one, princess?"

"Of course, my knight."

My knight...? That was even worse than *princess,*

QUALIFY, AND LIKELY HAS NOTHING TO DO WITH MUSTERING AT ALL. SO WHY MENTION IT? BECAUSE I WANT TO OFFER THIS INVALUABLE PIECE OF ADVICE FOR ALL WHO FIND THEMSELVES MUSTERING IN A MUSTER ROOM, OR INDEED WHO FIND THEMSELVES SHARING ANY SMALL SPACE WITH OTHER PEOPLE: IF YOU WANT TO CUT THE MUSTARD, PLEASE DON'T CUT THE CHEESE.

Brett thought. Couldn't they keep their pet names private?

Amber picked up a vest from a pile and handed it to Brett. "Here, honey."

"Thanks, orange is my favorite color," he said, unable to keep the sarcasm out of his voice. Amber had never been anything but nice to him—almost too nice—and yet he couldn't bring himself to like her.

Brett's father eyed the parfait glass in his hand. "Didn't you already have one of those Jell-O things this morning?"

"So? They're free."

"That's not the point. You haven't even had lunch yet. No wonder—" His father stopped himself before finishing his sentence.

"No wonder what?" Go on, thought Brett. Say it.

"Do you want to be like all the other overweight losers on this ship?" said his father, lowering his voice. He smiled broadly for the benefit of their fellow passengers.

"If that's how you feel, why did you buy this ship in the first place?" asked Brett, stung.

His father shrugged. "I like big things."

"Yeah, except for me," said Brett under his breath.

Brett senior's scalp reddened underneath his new hair plugs. "It doesn't matter whether *I* like you," he said, struggling to control his anger. "It only matters whether *you* like you."

Amber put one soothing hand on Brett's shoulder and one on his father's. "All your father is saying is that you need to take care of yourself," she cooed to Brett in her unnervingly sweet voice. "There are so many great exercise classes on the ship.... Pilates... Jazz-aerobics... Why don't you try one? Or at least go for a swim. Your father says you used to be a very strong swimmer."

"Yeah. Emphasis on *used to be*." Brett hadn't voluntarily taken his shirt off in public since he was ten. (Or, to be more exact, since the day Mitch Poll had started making fun of Brett's "boy boobs" at their class swim party.)

Mercifully, a neighboring passenger shushed them. A diagram of the ship was being projected onto a screen above the stage. Red circles were drawn around the lifeboats.

"In the unlikely event of an evacuation, you will be escorted to a tender. Do not attempt to board without a crew member...."*

The emergency training session had begun.

---

* FOR SUCH A SOFT AND DELICATE LITTLE WORD, *TENDER* HAS MANY MEANINGS. YOU MAY TREAT PEOPLE WITH TENDERNESS BECAUSE YOU FEEL TENDERLY TOWARD THEM, OR SIMPLY BECAUSE YOU ARE TENDER-HEARTED. IF YOU HAVE DONE A JOB, YOU SHOULD BE PAID IN LEGAL TENDER (I.E., MONEY). IF YOU AREN'T, I SUGGEST YOU TENDER YOUR RESIGNATION (I.E., QUIT). IF A SHIP IS TENDER, IT TIPS EASILY. LARGER SHIPS ARE USUALLY MORE STABLE, BUT THEY ARE LIKELY TO HAVE A TENDER OR TWO ABOARD. *A TENDER* IS A SMALL BOAT USED TO CONVEY PEOPLE OR THINGS BACK AND FORTH FROM A LARGER SHIP TO THE SHORE. ON

Brett's father was always buying things: oil rigs, construction companies, sports teams. Still, Brett had been a little surprised when his father announced that he had bought a cruise line. As far as Brett could remember, his father had never expressed much interest in sea vessels or even the sea itself, outside of extracting oil from underneath it.

Why buy an entire fleet of cruise ships?

But what had really surprised Brett was that his father wanted to take *him* on a cruise. In the old days, when his mother was still alive, they'd traveled all the time, but his father rarely took Brett away for a weekend anymore, never mind a weeklong vacation. Brett now suspected Amber's influence. She might not care much about Brett one way or the other, but at least she had some idea about the way families were supposed to behave.

Unlike his father.

He hates me, Brett thought. He really hates me.

His father had practically admitted it to his face.

After quitting the muster room, Brett found himself back on the Lido Deck. Another parfait. It was the only answer to the terrible pit that had opened in his stomach. But when he reached the

---

CRUISE SHIPS, TENDERS DOUBLE AS LIFEBOATS, AND IF ONE HAPPENS TO SAVE YOUR LIFE, I AM CERTAIN YOU WILL FEEL GREAT TENDERNESS FOR IT.

Snack Shack, it was closed. The dessert case was empty.

Now, *this* is an emergency, he thought.

As Brett considered his options—pizza? gelato? those twisty croissant-y things in the Tahiti Dining Room?—he noticed an open door next to the café. Inside was a gleaming stainless-steel world of counters and refrigerators and ovens and heat lamps. Standing in a corner, beckoning to Brett like a diamond necklace to a jewel thief, was a rolling rack stacked with Jell-O parfaits. Dozens of them. In every color. Each topped with a bright red maraschino cherry.

Glancing briefly at the STAFF ONLY sign, he walked straight through the door. The parfaits were free anyway, he reasoned. And if he got caught, well, his father owned the ship. Basically, he was stealing from himself.

He was in the middle of his second parfait— fourth if you counted the two he'd eaten earlier in the day—when a muffled noise caught his attention. It sounded like cars caught in traffic, honking and revving their motors, and it came from behind a steel door at the far end of the kitchen.

Above the door: a blinking red light and the words ACCESS RESTRICTED.

Ordinarily, Brett was a cautious fellow. True, he often spoke without thinking. He was especially bad at holding his tongue when he was being bullied (a twice- or thrice-daily occurrence). But when it came to serious risk taking, let's just say he preferred the comforts of a couch and a touch-screen device. Today was different. Maybe it was his anger at his father, maybe the Jell-O in his bloodstream, or maybe all that red dye in the cherries; whatever the reason, Brett felt bold and reckless. He inserted his all-access ID card into the slot.

Stepping through the door, he found himself at the top of a stairwell. At the bottom was an enormous storage area—a warehouse space that would have seemed large enough on land, let alone at sea—filled with boxes and crates of all shapes and sizes.

As soon as Brett walked in, he identified the source of the traffic sounds: not cars but animals. *Live* animals. Goats. Sheep. Pigs. Chickens. Even a few cows. All squeezed into pens. It looked as if an entire farmyard had been airlifted onto the ship.

It smelled like that, too.

Why animals on a cruise? For a petting zoo? Maybe a *tableau vivant* of Noah's Ark?* Brett didn't know anything about farming, but the animals sure didn't look happy.

---

* A *TABLEAU VIVANT* IS A "LIVING PICTURE" WHEREIN HUMAN—OR IN THIS CASE, *ANIMAL*—ACTORS POSE WITHOUT MOVING, STAGING A SCENE FROM HISTORY OR LITERATURE OR ART. JUST A MOMENT AGO, FOR EXAMPLE, WHEN I WAS SITTING AT MY DESK, STARING INTO SPACE, WITH A PEN FROZEN IN MY HAND, I DID NOT HAVE WRITER'S BLOCK; I WAS MERELY CREATING A TABLEAU VIVANT OF *L'ÉCRIVAIN AU TRAVAIL*. THAT'S "THE WRITER AT WORK" FOR YOU HELPLESS NON-FRANCOPHONES.

Behind them sat a rusted steel shipping container the size of a city bus, with airholes drilled into its sides. Next to the shipping container was a rack of fire extinguishers, as well as a locked glass case filled with weapons—stun guns, spearguns, rifles—enough to take down a blue whale or a herd of elephants.

No, probably not a petting zoo.

Suddenly, he heard people entering the room, arguing.

Trying not to panic, Brett stepped behind the shipping container and listened. A woman was complaining that the ship's crew was unhappy about having live animals in the hold. "They're smelly and only encourage the vermin!" Brett recognized her voice from the intercom.

"Not your business, lady," a man growled. "This space is off-limits to everyone except Mr. Perry and the staff of Operation St. George."

Brett swallowed. Mr. Perry was his father, Brett senior. The man who was speaking sounded like Mack, the ex-boxer who worked as his father's bodyguard and chauffeur. Brett peeked around the corner: Sure enough, Mack was there, and Brett's father, too. (Thankfully, his father was now wearing a Hawaiian shirt and tan pants. Not a great look, but Brett preferred it to the bathing suit.) Walking with them was a tall woman in uniform.

"I'm the captain of this ship, you moron," she said, incensed. "No space is off-limits to me!"

"And I'm the owner of this ship," Brett's father reminded her. "Your employer."

"I am still responsible for two thousand passengers. Never mind a thousand crew members. What is this 'Operation St. George'?"

Brett stepped back out of view. He couldn't risk his father seeing him now. He'd had more than enough parental disapproval for one day. The container door was open. He slipped inside—

What the...?

Bolted to the floor were a half dozen iron chains attached to an equal number of manacles. The chains looked so heavy and barbaric that at first Brett was sure they were fake. He thought of the magic show that was supposed to take place the following night. Could the chains be props for a Houdini-style escape routine? Perhaps the entire container was a magician's set—a cage for a stage.

Maybe the farm animals were part of the show, too?

Then Brett spied the massive steel muzzle on the floor. Leaning in for a closer look, he accidentally brushed against one of the chains. It clanged loudly against the side of the container.

Oops.

He held his breath. One...two...Silently, he

counted to himself, as if he were waiting for a bomb to explode. Three... four... Had he averted discovery?

Then—

"Brett!"

His father stared at him from the doorway, more furious than surprised.

"Um, hello," said Brett numbly.

The captain stepped up from behind Brett's father. "What in the world...?" Horrified, she stared not at Brett but at the contraption in front of his feet.

Brett glanced down again. The muzzle was a brutal piece of hardware, all right, made of steel thick enough to hold the biggest, strongest animal on earth. On the inside were spikes so long and so sharp, they would keep King Kong from opening his jaws.

This cage he'd stumbled into—it wasn't meant for a magician.

It was meant for a monster.

CHAPTER
TWO

CAPTURE THE VOG

If you've ever climbed a volcano, or even seen a picture of a volcano, you may have noticed the cloudy haze lingering in the nearby air. This haze is called *vog* (as in volcanic smog). Clay had been living under its spell for over six weeks, and still he couldn't get used to it.

Most mornings, and almost every evening, the fog rolled in from the ocean to meet the smoke rising from Mount Forge, Price Island's far-too-active (some might say hyperactive) volcano. Stirred together like ingredients in a mad laboratory experiment, the fog and smoke became the billowing clouds of vog that stung Clay's eyes and seared his throat. Of course, sometimes the vog didn't billow; it just crept around the island, like an invisible predator, and made him feel tired and irritable without his knowing why. And then there were the times, like today, when Mount

Forge acted up without warning, and all of a sudden the entire island was covered in a layer of vog so thick it was like someone had not only turned off the lights but turned off the gravity as well, giving him the sense of being suspended in a strange gray void.

Tucked away in a narrow valley, Clay's summer camp, Earth Ranch, usually escaped the worst of the vog, but that morning two cabinfuls of kids had left camp to spend the day at Bamboo Bay—a smallish U-shaped beach that backed up against a bamboo forest on one side and Mount Forge on the other. Unfortunately, as soon as they reached the beach, Mount Forge started belching smoke and vomiting lava as if the earth itself were suffering a terrible case of gastroenteritis. There was little danger of lava making it all the way down to the ocean, but, clearly, there would be no surfing or even any sunning today.

Flint, the junior counselor who was leading the beach expedition, suggested that the campers make the best of the bad weather by playing a game of Capture the Flag.

"We can call it Capture the Vog—it'll be awesome!"

He broke off a stick of bamboo. Then he looked up at the sky and released a tall plume of fire from his mouth, like a fire-breather at a carnival. All around him, the vog glowed orange and yellow, as if there'd been another volcanic eruption. When the fire subsided, a small flame burned at the end of the stick.

It was an impressive performance, made more so by the careless style of the performer. Flint had that cool-guy way of making tough things look easy.

As the campers applauded, he dragged his new torch across the beach, leaving a line of fire flickering in the black volcanic sand. A stranger might have guessed that he'd prepared ahead of time by pouring a line of gasoline, but his companions knew better. Flint had a special gift for pyrotechnics. He didn't need gas to light a fire; he needed only to snap his fingers.

In fact, many of the campers had talents like his, even if their skills were less advanced and their tricks less spectacular. Disguised as an outdoor survival camp for juvenile delinquents, Earth Ranch was, secretly, a magic camp for young adepts—a camp that depended on its remote location and ever-present vog for protection.

"Okay, Frogs, everything on this side of the line is yours," Flint declared, the flames turning his blue eyes gold. "Worms, the other side is yours." The Frogs were the younger girls, who resided in the cabin known as the Pond. The Worms were the younger boys, who resided in Earth Cabin—Clay's cabin. "Winners get to eat the losers' s'mores tonight. And don't forget—camp rules, everybody!"

"Yeah, except for you, right?" Clay scoffed.

Flint glared at him. "What did you say, Worm?"

Clay hid his smile. "Nothing!"

Camp rules meant No Magic.

The kids at Earth Ranch were forbidden from doing magic without adult supervision, but for some reason the rule never seemed to apply to Flint, despite his being only fifteen and not yet a full counselor. Certainly, it hadn't stopped him from making Clay's bunk smoke as if it were on fire when he passed by the previous night. Nor had it stopped him from making Clay's toothbrush start to melt that morning when he saw Clay brushing his teeth.

Someday, Clay had vowed, he would get Flint back.

Just...maybe not today.

"You have one minute to huddle, and then the game begins," Flint declared as he started walking down the beach. "I'll be back in ten to see the bloodbath!"

He started walking down the beach, alone.

The younger campers exchanged knowing glances. Flint had been disappearing a lot lately. The rumor was that he'd been practicing a new type of magic in secret. Nobody knew what this type of magic was, but it was undoubtedly difficult—and dangerous.

I don't know whether you've ever played Capture the Flag, but like most so-called recreational activities, it can quickly become very competitive.* In their pregame huddle, Clay's cabinmates, the Worms, strategized like they were plotting the crime of the century. No surprise, perhaps, given that they *were* criminals—or, rather, "struggling youth," as Earth Ranch called them in its glossy brochure.** Also, of course, they were magicians-in-training, but at Earth Ranch the campers tended to confuse crime with magic. Both things, after all, involved breaking laws—the one the laws of the land, the other the laws of nature.

Kwan, a Worm with a big, slick, swooping hairdo and a big, slick, swooping ego to match, elected himself team captain. He pointed toward a boy with a gold-tipped Afro and started giving orders. "Jonah, you're on recon. Scope out the opposition. When the target is vulnerable, give a sign."

Jonah nodded almost imperceptibly. Among his peers he was known to have a special knack for seeing things that others couldn't, whether in the future or in the dark. (It was an enviable skill because, unlike some other forms of magic, it could be practiced without attracting a counselor's attention.)

---

* Take dodgeball, for example. Or rather, don't take dodge-ball. The point of dodgeball is to dodge it entirely.
** In its brochure, the camp advertised itself as a place where kids "gained confidence through contact with the natural world," failing to mention that at Earth Ranch the natural world often appeared *super*natural.

Kwan turned to a second colorfully coiffed boy—this one with a green Mohawk. "Pablo, *mi amigo*, your job is to create a diversion."

Pablo furrowed his brow, considering. "Explosives?"

"Tempting," admitted Kwan. "But I'm thinking robotics. We could use another player on the team, even if it's not human."

"An automaton? But Flint said camp rules..." Pablo protested halfheartedly, even though his friends could see the gleam in his eye.

"Do you see any counselors?" said Kwan.

Pablo grinned. "How much time do I have?"

"About three minutes. Plenty for a man of your genius."

Kwan sounded sarcastic, but it was true: Pablo had a fantastic ability to make robotic creatures— automatons—from unlikely materials, in record time. Indeed, Pablo was already picking up stray bamboo sticks and strings of seaweed and manipulating them as if they were steel rods and copper wires.

"So here's the plan, my brother Worms," Kwan continued. "While Pablo's robo-man is distracting the enemy, I will secure the target. Then I will make a big show of passing off the flag to Pablo...."

Seemingly out of nowhere, a playing card appeared in Kwan's hand. He tossed it to Pablo, but by the time Pablo grabbed for it, the card had vanished into the air.

"But really, secretly, I will pass it off to Jonah, who will take it home and win those sweet, sweet s'mores for us...."

Jonah looked down. The card was in his hand. A joker. He shook his head. "Show-off."

The others laughed.

Kwan was a master of legerdemain and an expert swindler; his cabinmates knew better than to engage him in a serious game of poker or even a friendly game of gin rummy.* If anybody could steal a flag and then pass it off to someone else a second later, Kwan could.

"Anything I can do?" asked Clay, as casually as he could. (He didn't want to come off like the last kid picked in a game of kickball, even if he felt a little bit that way.) "I know I've never robbed a bank like the rest of you reprobates—but I think I know how to play Capture the Flag."

"What are you talking about, dude? You're our MVP!" Kwan patted Clay on the head. "You protect our flag, and, uh, tag any girl who crosses onto our side and take her to jail, which is, um, that boulder

---

* LEGERDEMAIN MEANS "SLEIGHT OF HAND" AND REFERS MAINLY TO CLOSE-UP MAGIC LIKE CARD AND COIN TRICKS. IT'S TRUE, I'VE NEVER BEEN ESPECIALLY SKILLED AT LEGERDEMAIN MYSELF, BUT I LIKE TO PRACTICE WHEN I'M WRITING, AND I'M GETTING MUCH BETTER, I THINK. EVEN AS THIS SENTENCE IS BEING TYPED, I AM HOLDING A COIN BETWEEN MY FINGERS. TALK ABOUT DEXTERITY! NO, I DON'T TYPE MY OWN BOOKS— THEY ARE DICTATED—BUT THAT IS A MINOR QUIBBLE, IS IT NOT?

over there." Kwan, who fancied himself a ladies' man, wiggled his eyebrows mischievously. "See, you have the best job in the game—guarding the girls!"

Clay laughed and shook his head. "You're a Neanderthal.

"So where's our flag, anyway?" he asked.

"Here—" Kwan pulled a long white tube sock off his foot and held it up. The bottom was dirty and moist, and the surrounding air suddenly swirled with eau de toe.

Clay recoiled. "Ugh! Dude, that's gross."

"Exactly," said Kwan, laughing. "It's like a protection spell—nobody will want to touch it!" He wagged the sock in front of Clay's face, and Clay dove away.

They all did.

In a matter of minutes, the game had begun and Clay was manning his post. Next to him, Kwan's sock hung limply from a stick, an uninspiring—and very stinky—flag, but Clay dutifully guarded it nonetheless.

It was eerily silent. Not having Jonah's extraordinary talent for seeing in the dark—or in this case, the vog—Clay couldn't see what the others were doing, but as far as he could tell, events were proceeding according to plan. Maybe the Worms would win without his coming into contact with another player.

Or did silence mean bad news rather than good? Whenever Clay felt antsy, his knee jiggled up and down. His knee was already jiggling uncontrollably when he heard muffled screams and saw a strange, hairy silhouette moving jerkily in the vog. It looked like a scarecrow that was losing its stuffing, and it lurched in one direction and then another, as if it were hunting for wayward crows or maybe for a human brain to steal as its own.

Clay tensed as the creature staggered toward him.

What was it?

Just as Clay was considering running for his life, one of the thing's arms fell off. It took another step forward, then collapsed in a heap.

Oh! So that's what it was.

Clay exhaled, relieved and impressed. Pablo was a true wizard when it came to automatons. If his sticks-and-seaweed robo-man could spook Clay, who was expecting it, it must have been terrifying to the unsuspecting Frogs—a successful diversion. With any luck, Jonah would soon be crossing back to their side with the Frogs' flag in hand.

"Clay! Over here!" a familiar voice called in singsong, from somewhere to his right. "Catch me if you can!"

Leira.

It figured that the Frogs would send her for the boys' flag. If anybody was a better thief than Kwan, it was Leira, master pickpocket and perennial prankster.

She was the person Clay liked best at camp, but also the person who irritated him the most. He couldn't count how many times she had stolen his wallet just for a laugh.

Clay hesitated. It would be very satisfying to take her out of the game and throw her into jail. Should he look for her? Or should he be cautious and keep guarding the flag?

He leaped into the vog, toward where he had heard Leira's voice come from. "Got you!"

As soon as he grabbed her sleeve, he knew he'd fallen into a trap; it had been far too easy to catch her.

In the end, it wasn't even Leira whom he'd caught. It was her sister, Mira, laughing gleefully.

"No, I got *you!*" she said in her natural voice, which was a little higher-pitched and a lot snottier than her sister's. "Hope you're not too disappointed."

Mira was an actress and was well known at camp for her uncannily accurate impersonations of the other campers. She could fool you into thinking she was almost anyone. Normally, Leira hated it when Mira imitated her; she must have made an exception for the sake of the game.

"Don't tell me," said Clay, the horrible truth sinking in. "If you're here, that means Leira is—"

"Crossing back onto our side with your flag just about now?" Mira gloated. "Uh-huh."

Sure enough, they heard her sister hooting in

victory. "And—*BOOM!*—she takes it over the line!" Leira shouted. "Watch and learn, boys!"

A second later, she cried out, laughing, "Oh, man, this sock stinks!"

The girls had won.

"Frogs rule! Worms stink!" they chanted. "We get dessert! The Worms eat dirt!"

"C'mon, time to face your humiliation," said Mira.

"Go ahead," said Clay. "I'll be there in a second."

Clay sat down on the rock that had been designated the Worms' jail, unable to believe he'd fallen for such a simple trick. Not only could he not build an automaton or see in the dark or start a fire with a snap or do any of the other extraordinary things that the other kids at camp could do, he couldn't even keep his eye on a smelly sock.

His cabinmates would never let him live this down.

Not for the first time, Clay wondered why his older brother, Max-Ernest, had gone to so much trouble to get him into this camp.* His brother seemed to have faith that Clay would make a good

---

* As you can read in my previous book, *Bad Magic*, if you're curious (or if you just want to impress me), Clay's road to Earth Ranch began with a graffiti mural bearing his signature, which appeared inexplicably on a wall at his school. As it turned out, this was only the first in a long series of not-so-accidental events that culminated in his indoctrination into the mysteries of Price Island. What parts of his journey his brother had a direct hand in Clay didn't know; but that his brother had a hand in some of them Clay knew for certain.

magician, just because they used to do magic shows together when Clay was little. But at Earth Ranch, whatever being a magician was, it wasn't about coin tricks or pulling bunnies out of hats.

Unfortunately, Clay had no way to ask Max-Ernest about magicians or bunnies or anything else. Clay didn't know where his brother was—only that he was off somewhere fighting to protect some magical "Other Side" that Clay couldn't see and barely understood. According to Max-Ernest, Clay would soon very likely become caught up in this mysterious battle himself.

Clay only hoped he could be more useful in a battle for the fate of the magical universe than in a game of Capture the Flag.

When Clay stood up, he felt a little dizzy, but he ignored it. The vog had gotten thicker, that was all.

He started walking in the direction Mira had gone (or the direction he *thought* she had gone), only to realize he was walking into the ocean. Feet wet, he backtracked, but he became confused again after taking a few soggy steps onto dry sand.

The vog was now so dense that he was having trouble breathing, and he could barely see his own hands. He dropped to the sand and crawled for a moment because the air was a little better below knee level.

Soon he found himself at the base of Mount Forge, maneuvering between boulders. There wasn't a trail exactly, but he discovered that if he walked very slowly, he was able to avoid falling. He would worry about the others later, he decided; he just wanted to get out of the vog.

After hiking for almost thirty minutes—and traveling a distance that would have normally taken five minutes—Clay hoisted himself up a final boulder and stood on level ground. Wisps of steam rose from a hole in the rocks a few feet away, but Clay took little notice; there were volcanic steam vents all over the island. Otherwise, the air was significantly clearer up here than it had been below.

It was as good a place as any to wait out the vog.

In his backpack, alongside the notebook in which he practiced his graffiti art, he had a water bottle, trail mix, and a flashlight. He could easily survive here for a few hours, or even a day or two if need be. The counselors drilled it into the campers to keep emergency supplies with them at all times. You never knew what was going to happen on Price Island; it was best to be prepared.*

Clay was debating his next move when he

---

* IN THIS WAY, EARTH RANCH REMINDED CLAY OF THE OLD DAYS, WHEN HIS BROTHER'S SURVIVALIST FRIEND CASS USED TO QUIZ CLAY DAILY ON WHAT TO DO IN CASE OF DISASTER.

saw somebody walk out of a narrow crevice in the mountainside.

Instinctively, Clay ducked behind a boulder and hid, his body tense. As far as he knew, there were no inhabitants on the island outside of Earth Ranch, and yet it seemed unlikely that any of the other campers would have made it up the mountain in the vog.

After catching his breath, Clay peeked out:

It was Flint!

What was *he* doing here?

The older boy looked around, as if to make sure he wasn't being observed, and then headed in Clay's direction.

Clay hugged his side of the boulder, waiting until he was sure Flint had passed. He was suddenly very curious to see what was behind that crevice.

Not quite as narrow as it had looked from a distance, the crevice was actually the entrance to a large cave—large enough to hold at least four or five cars.

The light was dim inside, and at first Clay couldn't see anything but rock, but when he turned on his flashlight, he realized that the cave walls were covered with paintings. They were obviously very old—ancient, even—and resembled primitive cave paintings he'd seen in books.

A few of the paintings showed men hunting with spears or bows and arrows, and one showed

a dozen men rowing a long boat of some kind. But the most striking paintings depicted—both singly and in groups—dark winged creatures with long red tongues. Some of these creatures carried deer or other animals in their claws. Others circled a smoking volcano that bore a more-than-passing resemblance to Mount Forge.

It was difficult to tell what, specifically, the flying beasts were meant to represent, but there was a distinct reptilian quality to their sharp claws and curling tails. Could they be dinosaurs? Clay wondered. What were those flying dinosaurs called? When he was ten years old, he would have known the answer.

Nowadays, his interests ran to other things, like skateboards and graffiti art. Looking at the cave paintings, he had an impulse to draw something on the cave walls himself, though of course he resisted. (I hope it goes without saying that he would never deface the natural environment!) He remembered his mother once comparing the cave paintings at Lascaux to graffiti.* At the time, he had dismissed the idea as silly—just his mother's way of trying to make

---

* LASCAUX IS A CAVE IN SOUTHWESTERN FRANCE THAT CONTAINS PAINTINGS FROM THE PALEOLITHIC ERA. MORE THAN 17,000 YEARS AGO, ANCIENT ARTISTS DREW PEOPLE, ANIMALS, LANDSCAPES, AND ABSTRACT DOODLES ON THE CAVE'S WALLS (MUCH AS MODERN HUMANS DO ON THEIR ARMS). THESE PAINTINGS ARE STILL VISIBLE TODAY, THOUGH THE PUBLIC HAS BEEN BANNED FROM THE SITE FOR OVER FIFTY YEARS, EVER SINCE

Clay's enthusiasms fit into her own. Now he wasn't so sure. Maybe there was a real basis for the comparison.

Telling stories on a wall. That's what cave painting was. That's what graffiti was.

Clay pointed his flashlight beam on one painting after another, with the idea that he might copy one or two in his notebook. But as he delved deeper into the cave, he noticed that he'd become—suddenly—very, very sleepy.

Trying to fight this unexpected drowsiness, he took a few steps toward the cave entrance—then collapsed onto the stone floor as if he'd been shot with a tranquilizer gun. His flashlight beam landed on the biggest of the mysterious winged creatures, which appeared to be swooping down on one of the hunters. Struggling to keep his eyes open, Clay noticed that the creature's tongue was not only long and red but also oddly shaped; instead of coming to a point at the end, or even forking like a snake's, the tongue spread wider as it got farther from the creature's mouth—and closer to the hunter's head.

Wait, that's not a tongue at all, Clay thought, falling asleep.

That's *fire*.

THOUSANDS OF VISITORS BREATHED ALL OVER THE ARTWORK, DESTROYING IN A FEW WEEKS WHAT HAD PREVIOUSLY LASTED FOR MILLENNIA.

Another cave, deeper underground. It is dark, but the rock walls are encrusted with crystals. They reflect the fiery glow of lava.

Clay is leaning over the edge of a lava pit. It is like a furnace. The heat sears his face.

As he watches, patches of lava harden into black crust, only to be swallowed by ripples of red-hot molten rock. Sulfurous gases bubble up like farts in some monstrous bathtub, filling the cave with their stench. And a stray leaf floats up and down in the heat. It catches fire just before touching the lava's surface.

Suddenly, Clay is aware of a new feeling in his stomach. It bubbles inside him like the sulfur—a deep, powerful urge to dive in.

To swim in the lava.

With horror, he realizes that he has leaned in too far. He struggles to stay upright. Too late!

Terrified, he tumbles into the pit, and...

It is as if he is plunging into a spring. Hot, yes—but wonderfully hot. He sinks deeper and deeper, luxuriating in the thick, gurgling, life-giving lava. He has never felt so good. Nothing burns him. It couldn't. It is inside him, as if he has somehow become the fire itself.

He wants to stay under forever.

Then, just as he thinks he must be nearing the center of the earth, he flips himself around. With strength he didn't know he possessed, he pushes himself upward. Faster and faster he rises until he erupts from the crater of the volcano, riding a geyser of molten rock.

Still he does not stop.

Smoke mushrooming behind him, he rockets into the starry night sky.

Soon the volcano is just a dot on that spinning blue-and-green egg called Planet Earth.

With a fiery roar, he spreads his wings and flies.

CHAPTER
THREE

BEACHED

The first thing Clay noticed when he awoke was the smell. It was worse than Kwan's socks. Worse even than his school bus on the way home from burrito day in the cafeteria.

It was a rotten-egg sort of smell, and it was coming from somewhere deep in the bowels of the mountain. Where had he smelled it before? In his dream. That was it. It all came back in a flash. Such an intense dream. Almost unconsciously, he rolled his shoulders as if they were wings. If only he could really fly like that.

Holding his nose, he stood up and took a last look around at the cave paintings.

Dragons.

Of course, they were dragons. He couldn't believe he hadn't seen it right away.

The paintings probably depicted a myth or legend,

like the story of the creation of the volcano or the discovery of fire. And yet to Clay's artist eye, the dragons looked surprisingly lifelike, as if the paintings were showing scenes not from an ancient myth but from a recent hunt.

Strange.

He was about to step outside when he spied a square object sitting in the shadows next to the cave entrance.

When he picked it up, he saw that it was a book. It was largish, the size of a school notebook, and bound in some kind of tough, scaly hide or skin that had cracked and yellowed over time, like an old man's toenail. Inside, there was a manuscript written on parchment paper, with a title scrawled across the top page in black ink:

Secrets of the Occulta Draco
or,
The Memoirs of a Dragon Tamer
AD 1600

Tucked into the book was a slip of paper with a library call number penciled on it. Even if there hadn't been a call number, Clay would have known where the book came from: the private book collection called (misleadingly) the Price Public Library. Campers, and even counselors, were only occasionally allowed to enter the library, and they were never allowed to remove books. Flint must have hidden the book in the cave so that nobody would see that he'd taken it.

Naturally, Clay was curious to read whatever was written inside, but there was no time for that now. He debated for only a moment before putting the book in his backpack. Returning it to the library would be a good deed.

Making Flint angry and confused when he came back to look for it? Even better!

By the time Clay got to the beach, the vog was gone and the ocean shimmered in the afternoon sun. He thought it must be about three or four o'clock, but he couldn't be sure. He'd slept for at least a couple of hours.

"Hello?" he called out. "Anybody here?"

There was no answer.

He walked along the beach, looking for his friends, but as far as he could tell, everybody had left without him. Maybe they'd figured he went back to camp? Or were his cabinmates getting back at him for losing the game of Capture the Flag?

If one of them had gone missing, he definitely would have waited, he thought.

Well, almost definitely...

Clay stopped in his tracks.

Yuck.

About twelve feet ahead, there was a big white lump lying on the black sand. At first, Clay took it for a squid washed up on the beach, or maybe just a very large, very pale jellyfish. Whatever it was, it was disgusting. (Clay had inherited from his brother a fear of anything white and slimy—chiefly mayonnaise.) And probably dead.

Still, Clay thought, he should take a closer look—just in case it was a live seal or baby whale or other animal that needed to be pushed back into the sea.

Only a little—well, a lot—nervous, he stepped up to the mysterious lump...

. . . and stared in surprise.

It wasn't a squid or a jellyfish or a seal or a whale; it was a boy, a boy who looked to be about Clay's age and who was tangled in seaweed and dripping seawater, as if he had only recently washed up onshore. The boy's hair was full of sand, and his eyes were crusted with salt. His wet shirt had come unbuttoned, revealing a soft, plump belly, and his equally wet pants were torn and bunched up around the knees. He had lost his shoes and one of his socks. Only his black bow tie showed no sign of having been tossed and turned by the ocean; it was still shiny and perfectly tied around his neck. Until—

"Aack!" Clay yelped, startled.

The bow tie had moved! For a second he thought the boy had awakened, but then he saw the little purple crab scurrying away across the sand.

Clay's heart pounded. He had no idea what to do.

Calm down, Clay told himself. First things first.

"Hey, um, can you hear me?" Clay managed to ask, his voice hoarse.

No reply.

Starting to sweat, Clay knelt by the boy's side and put his hand on the boy's cheek. It was cold and clammy.

But was it *dead* clammy? Or just *clammy*?

He lifted the boy's wrist and felt for a pulse. He

didn't feel one, but that didn't mean anything; he hardly knew what a pulse should feel like.

He tried to remember what he knew about CPR; it wasn't much. You were supposed to push on the person's chest—or was it the stomach? And then you were supposed to count to something. And then there was the mouth-to-mouth part.

Yikes.

He tried pushing the boy's chest a couple of times.

Nothing.

Desperate, he shook the boy by the shoulders. "Wake up! I mean, if you're alive..."

Suddenly, a spray of spit and salt water and vomit hit Clay in the face. He wiped the warm, sour mess off his nose and cheek, almost as relieved as he was disgusted. It was the first time he'd been happy to have somebody throw up on him. Not that anybody had ever thrown up on him before.

When the boy's coughing subsided, he opened an eye and squinted at Clay.

"Don't tell me—some kid beat me up again," he said groggily. "Was it you?"

"What? No! I don't even know you."

"Then why does my head hurt so bad?" the boy demanded. "And why are you grabbing my shoulder like that?"

"Because...Never mind." Embarrassed, Clay let go.

"Wait, I'm not at school, am I?" Confused, the boy pushed himself up to a sitting position. He rubbed his eyes and looked around, blinking. "I guess this is one of those good-news-bad-news situations, huh?"

"You really don't know where you are?" Was it possible the boy was as surprised to find himself here as Clay was?

The boy shook his head. "No idea...unless..." He looked suspiciously at Clay. "Am I on a reality show?"

Clay laughed. "Not that I know of. Unless... are you?" In truth, it was just as likely as any other explanation for the boy's mysterious appearance on the beach.*

"I don't think so....Do you have any water? My mouth is burning."

Clay handed over his water bottle. The boy looked at the bottle with distaste—it *was* pretty dirty, now that Clay saw it from someone else's perspective—then took a swig.

"Well, it's not Perrier, but it'll do in a pinch," the boy said, wiping his mouth.

---

* OF COURSE, ANOTHER POSSIBILITY WAS THAT THE EVENT HAD BEEN STAGED FOR CLAY'S BENEFIT. HIS INITIATION AT EARTH RANCH HAD INVOLVED AN ELABORATE, WEEKS-LONG CHARADE THAT MADE HIM QUESTION ALL LEVELS OF REALITY, BUT HE'D BEEN ASSURED THAT THE INITIATION WAS OVER, AND SO FAR HE'D HAD NO REASON TO DOUBT IT.

He handed back the bottle. "Okay, so tell me—where are we? Guam? Tahiti? Indonesia?"

"No, just Price Island...and I'm Clay, by the way."

"Price—are you sure?" said the boy doubtfully. "I've never heard of it, and I've been to a ton of places. I'm Brett Perry. You know, like Perry International...?"

"Not really."

"Offshore drilling, war-zone security, military scandals...doesn't ring a bell?"

Clay shook his head. "Sorry."

"Oh." The boy—Brett—sounded surprised. Apparently, his family was famous—in his mind, at least. "Well, anyway, that's me. Or my dad, really. I'm Brett *junior.*"

Clay decided to change the subject. "You think maybe you were in a plane crash—I mean, if you travel so much?"

"Maybe..."

Brett reached for the bottle and took another swig of water—and coughed again.

"No, I remember now!" A shadow seemed to fall across his face, but he shrugged it off. "I was on a ship. A huge cruise ship. HUGE. Like a Las Vegas hotel."

"I've never been to Las Vegas."

"Wow. You are sheltered, aren't you? Well, the hotels there are ridiculously big, and so was the ship I was on. It had pools, a casino, everything." Brett's face brightened. "And the most amazing Jell-O parfaits ever! I know, Jell-O, who cares, right? But trust me, you have to try them. It's all about the combination of taste and texture."

Clay smiled uncertainly. Jell-O seemed like a funny thing to talk about under the circumstances. "Not sure I'm going on any cruises, but if I do—okay. How'd you wind up in the water?"

"Oh, I, uh, was running on the deck and I just... fell over the railing. Then I...I don't know, floated here?"

Clay had the impression that Brett was leaving something out of the story, but Clay didn't say anything. It wasn't in his nature to pry.

"Is there anything to eat in that backpack, by any chance?" Brett asked. "I'm so hungry I'm going to die."

Clay dug into his backpack and pulled out a handful of trail mix.

Brett made a face. "No offense, but I wouldn't feed that to my worst enemy's pet gerbil. Don't you have any anything else?"

Clay shook his head. This guy had nearly drowned, and he was complaining about trail mix? "Sorry. There's other stuff at camp."

"Oh, all right, then—" Brett grabbed the trail mix and threw it all into his mouth at once as if it were some terrible-tasting medicine.

"What camp?" he asked, his mouth full of nuts and raisins.

"Earth Ranch. My summer camp. So, uh, are you okay? Can you walk?"

"I guess." Brett picked a stray sunflower seed off his arm and ate it. Then he wobbled to his feet.

"Ugh. Head rush," he said, putting his hand to his forehead.

Clay regarded him skeptically. The guy didn't look like much of a hiker—under the best of circumstances. "Maybe I should go back and get help."

"No!" said Brett, as if Clay had proposed amputating a limb.

"You sure?"

"Isn't there a hotel or a resort or something?"

"Nope. Only camp. There's nothing else on the island."

"Seriously?" Brett looked alarmed. "Well, I can't go there."

Incredulous, Clay glanced around the beach. "What are you going to do? Swim home?"

Brett grabbed Clay by the arm and looked at him intently—*intensely* intently. "What do you think they'll do if you take me to your camp?"

"I don't know," said Clay, pulling away. Why was this kid freaking out? "Call your dad, I guess?"

"Exactly!"

"He's that bad?"

Brett nodded.

"Worse than being stranded on an island in the middle of nowhere?"

Brett nodded again.

"What about your mom?"

"Dead."

"Oh, jeez. Sorry," said Clay. Why couldn't there be anything simple about this situation?

"I never even knew her.... Now promise you won't tell anyone about me."

"Maybe if you explained...?" Clay suggested. "The director of the camp, Mr. Bailey—he's pretty cool."

"Please," scoffed Brett. "It's a summer camp. He'll turn me over to the authorities before I finish dinner. The only thing he's worried about is a lawsuit. Trust me, I know. My father's been in court more times than I can count."

Actually, Clay thought, what Mr. B would be most worried about is an outsider finding out about the true, magical nature of the camp. Maybe it would be best not to drag Brett to camp after all.

"Okay," said Clay. "So what do you want to do, then?"

"I need to think. Can't you just...wait?"

"Here? If I don't go back soon, they'll come looking for me for sure," said Clay.

At least, he hoped they would. He was still a

little sore about his friends going back to camp without him.

"So you're just going to leave me? You can't!" said Brett. He seemed almost as upset about the prospect of being left alone as he'd been about the prospect of being taken to camp.

Clay gripped his hair in exasperation. "What else am I supposed to do?"

"Oh, I don't know, maybe what any decent human being would do? Help me find more food, water, a place to sleep...shoes." Brett looked down at his bare foot. "Or leave me alone to wither away and die. Your choice."

Clay sighed. He had the feeling that his life on Price Island was about to become considerably more complicated.

"Okay, I know a place," he said reluctantly. "It smells kinda rank, but you'll be fine." Clay told Brett about the cave and how to get there. He didn't mention the dream—or the book.

Brett looked like he was about to protest, then thought better of it.

"Just promise not to tell anyone about me," he repeated. "Or I really will be dead."

He sounded so worried that an awful idea occurred to Clay:

What if Brett's fall from the cruise ship hadn't been an accident?

Prologus

Today, there are very few dragons left. Soon there may be none. Already, many people believe that dragons never existed.

I, the last of the Dragon Tamers, have decided to record my memories and to relate whatever wisdom I may have gained during a lifetime spent among the noblest and most magical of beasts, in the hope that one day, when dragons again roam the earth, a brave young person will read my words and will heed the dragon's call.

To that person, I dedicate this book.

But first, a word of caution: Only someone who has the true spirit of the Dragon Tamer may learn our ways. We speak the tongue of dragons, and that is not a language that can be taught, only awakened. One knows it instinctively, the

---

* PLEASE NOTE: I HAVE ABRIDGED AND MODERNIZED THIS SEVENTEENTH-CENTURY TEXT FOR EASE OF READING—AND ALSO TO ENSURE THAT SOME OF THE MORE SENSITIVE INFORMATION IN THE MANUSCRIPT REMAINS SECRET.

way a great musician knows music, or one knows it not at all.

To all others, our words are gibberish, our traditions senseless, and our beliefs unfathomable.

Thus the secrets of our order, the Occulta Draco, are protected from those who would make mischief.

Alas, there are a few who share our knowledge of dragontongue yet have no love for dragonkind, or indeed for humankind. They have the gifts of a Dragon Tamer but not the heart. Inside their chests is nothing but an unquenchable hunger for dragonfire and the power it brings.

From these people, whom we call the Fire Breathers, this book must be kept at all costs. Were even one of them to learn its secrets, disaster would surely fall.

For he who has power over dragons has power over us all.

CHAPTER
FOUR

THE RAINBOW

Earth Ranch had a rainbow.

It was a permanent camp fixture, like the yurts and the geodesic dome and the lakefront rope swing. Sometimes it got a little brighter or dimmer. Sometimes it moved a little this way or that way. But rain or shine, it never left. Even in the vog it was there, lighting up the smoky air like a big neon sign.

According to the counselors, the rainbow acted as a sort of magical barometer. If and when it disappeared, they would know magic was in trouble. And yet for Clay, the rainbow's presence was far more frustrating than comforting. At this very moment, for example, as he was eating breakfast in front of Big Yurt (the closest thing Earth Ranch had to a dining hall), the rainbow appeared five or six feet away at the most, but he knew perfectly well that it would evaporate if he tried to touch it. No matter how tantalizingly close it came, the rainbow remained forever out of reach.

Just like magic itself.

Jonah waved his hand in front of Clay's face. "Stop staring. That thing will drive you crazy. Trust me, I chased it for six hours straight once."

Sitting across the table, Kwan laughed. "He's just tweaked that we left him on the beach yesterday."

"Wait, what?" said Clay, snapping out of it. Left who on the beach? Were they talking about Brett?

"You think we were so mad about Capture the Flag that we would leave you there on purpose?" said Pablo. "Okay, we're jerks sometimes, yeah, but c'mon—"

"We told you, it wasn't up to us," said Jonah. "We were all, *But what about Clay?* And Flint was like, *No worries, Clay went back to camp.*"

No, there was no way they could know about Brett, Clay reassured himself.

"Man, that guy really hates on you," said Kwan, shaking his head. "Flint's not going to be happy until your butt is off this island."

"Thanks," said Clay. "That makes me feel much better."

He took a sip of his carrot-beet juice and put it right down. Why did all the food in this hippie fairyland taste the same?

"Here, this will cheer you up," said Pablo, grabbing Clay's glass. He inserted his straw and started blowing bubbles.

"What are you doing?!"

"Watch—" Pablo withdrew his straw. The red-orange juice continued to bubble and fizz like carbonated soda.

Magic carbonated soda.

Clay smiled. "Cool. Radioactive spit."

He put the glass to his lips, then stopped mid-sip; the Pond counselor, Adriana, who happened to be the strictest counselor at the camp, was walking by. If she witnessed Pablo's magical tomfoolery, their whole table would be punished. She gave the boys a suspicious glance but continued on.

There was no chance for Clay to be relieved, however, because the bubbles were coming faster and faster.

"Oh, man—"

By the time he put his glass down, foam was spilling out of the glass, and juice was pouring out of his nose. He was drenched.

The others burst out laughing.

Pablo grinned. "Okay, so maybe I was a little mad that we had to give our s'mores to the girls last night...."

Juice dripping from his chin, Clay shook his head, laughing with them. "Yeah, well, you can just go...*expel-your-anus!*"

More laughter. *Expel-your-anus* was the Worms' favorite all-purpose rejoinder—not a real magic spell, perhaps, but almost as satisfying.* Pablo gamely put his hand to his mouth and made loud farting noises.

As he wiped himself off, Clay looked down at his plate. "Hey, what happened to my bananas?"

"Were you looking for these?" Laughing, a certain freckle-faced girl in a newsboy cap plopped three bananas onto his plate.

Of course.

Clay shook his head. "The master thief strikes again!"

"Why do you need three bananas, anyway?" asked Leira, sitting down next to him on the stone bench. "You think juggling fruit is that special magical talent you've been looking for?"

"They're for Como."

Como C. Llama was the llama Clay had been taking care of since his first day at camp. Hopefully, Leira wouldn't remember that Como hated bananas.

"Oh well," said Leira. "I didn't think you were the circus type anyway. Something will come along, you'll see. One day, you'll be picking your nose, and suddenly—"

---

* I BELIEVE THE PHRASE *EXPEL-YOUR-ANUS* WAS MEANT TO BE A JOCULAR REFERENCE TO *EXPELLIARMUS*, THE DISARMING SPELL IN A WELL-KNOWN SERIES OF CHILDREN'S BOOKS. HOWEVER, YOU MAY REST ASSURED THAT I DO NOT FIND THE REFERENCE FUNNY IN THE SLIGHTEST.

Clay grinned. "So *that's* how you became a pickpocket!"

Leira laughed ruefully. "I deserved that."

"Uh-oh—" She pointed to a bee hovering nearby. "Looks like somebody heard about your face fountain."

As the kids watched nervously, the first bee was joined by a small swarm of his brother drones. They spread out into a ribbon and then fluidly formed a question mark.

"Tell Buzz not to get all bent out of shape," said Kwan to the bees. "Whatever Adriana thinks she saw, it was only carrot juice."

Buzz was the Worm counselor and the camp beekeeper—or, as the campers sometimes joked, the Worm keeper and the bee counselor. Around camp, the bees served as his eyes and ears and, occasionally, as his message bearers.

The bees hovered in place, as if considering a rebuttal, then flew away with an angry hum.

"It's like we live in a prison run by bees," grumbled Pablo, who, as a self-described anarchist, hated authority of all kinds. "I swear, one day I'm going to zap those little spies with a can of bug spray."

Leira looked at him, aghast. "Don't even joke about that!"

"Sorry, forgot you were a vegan."

"That has nothing to do with it!"

Clay nervously patted his sweatshirt pocket with his juice-sticky fingers. Inside, the bananas sat next to a mango, one of the camp's homemade breakfast bars (dates, sunflower seeds, and bee pollen), and a worn pair of flip-flops. He hoped the pollen wouldn't attract the bees' attention.

Far from being a prison, Earth Ranch more closely resembled a preschool: All the campers ran around with bare feet and dirty faces; they did plenty of arts and crafts (magical arts and crafts, but nonetheless...); and there was circle time each morning and each afternoon. The afternoon circle, known simply as Circle, was the time for sharing feelings and airing concerns— in other words, for shouting and fighting. The morning circle, called Morning Mindfulness, was a calmer affair, akin to a yoga class—if your yoga instructor happened to be a wizard with a peculiar affection for bees.

That morning, Buzz sat on the ground under the dome, his long legs crossed in lotus position. A lone bee sat on his bushy mustache while others circled his head in a moving halo.

The campers sat facing him, their legs also crossed, but only Adriana, who was sitting in the back, keeping an eye on everyone from behind, was flexible enough to match Buzz's full lotus.

As for Clay, he wasn't quite sure what mindfulness was except that it was his idea of torture.* Never mind that there was a starving fugitive waiting for him in a cave. Unfortunately, Buzz had refused to excuse Clay from that morning's session, even when Clay had tried to insist that an early-morning hike would do him just as much good.

"Be aware of your breath..." Buzz was saying, his voice low and lulling. "Feel it, don't force it. Let your breath breathe you...."

As their counselor spoke, his breath became visible in puffs, as on a frosty winter day.

"There is no inhale, no exhale. There is only the ebb and flow of energy...."

One by one, the kids lit up in delighted surprise: Their breath was materializing in the air as well.

Unable to focus on his own breathing—unable to focus on anything at all, really—Clay watched the little clouds floating out of his friends' mouths. He glanced over his shoulder. Adriana gave him a look, and he turned back around.

From his own mouth, naturally, came nothing.

"This energy, this vital life force, the ancient Greeks called it *pneuma*—the breath of life."

---

* HONESTLY, I'M NOT SURE WHAT *MINDFULNESS* IS, EITHER. DOES IT HAVE SOMETHING TO DO WITH MEDITATION? (I MUST MEDITATE ON THE QUESTION.) *MINDLESSNESS*, ON THE OTHER HAND...I'M SORRY, WHAT WAS I SAYING?

Lingering in the air, the campers' breath curled like smoke. Gradually, it started to sparkle, as if it were made of gold dust.

Mesmerized, Clay began to relax. Finally, he could see his own breath, streaming from his mouth in one long exhale. He smiled to himself; maybe he had some magical potential after all.

"In Chinese medicine, it is *chi*. In the Hindu religion and in yoga, it is *prana*. But you are probably more familiar with what those famous yoga masters Obi-Wan Kenobi and Yoda call it—*the Force*."

The campers giggled uncomfortably, uncertain whether Buzz was joking. (Probable answer: He was and he wasn't.)

Above them, their golden breath spread out like a blanket, darkening the space beneath the geodesic dome while at the same time sparkling brighter and brighter. Soon, the campers were looking up at a night sky, replete with twinkling stars, swirling galaxies, and fiery comets.

"This energy, this *pneuma-prana-chi-force*, it is everywhere and nowhere. It is part of the unseen universe. The universe that we in the SOS call the Other Side."

At the mention of the Other Side, the stars, like so many golden snowflakes, started gently to fall. There were audible sighs from the campers.

"When the Other Side intersects with *our* side,

when we see its energy at work in the physical world—this we call magic."

As the last of the stars fell away, Buzz, still in lotus position, floated in the air, about two feet off the ground.

"And this I call the *flotus* position," he said, smiling.

Some of the kids laughed. Others rolled their eyes.

"Bad pun, I know, but there's a point to it. Magic, like yoga, is a practice. A practice we must maintain if we are to keep it from falling into the wrong hands. Perhaps I imagined it, but this morning the rainbow looked a bit... I'm sorry, give me a second—"

A bee hovered by Buzz's ear. Buzz frowned as he listened.

"Guys, I'm sorry, we have to cut this short," he said, lowering himself to the ground. "A cruise ship has anchored close to shore. I don't know if they're stopping for a snorkel, or if they're in some kind of distress, or if... well, better not to speculate."

The campers looked at one another in surprise. Nobody had heard of a boat ever stopping anywhere near the island. It was too remote and inhospitable for tourists, and the vog kept away even the most intrepid fishermen.

Clay tried not to show any reaction—

"Clay, are you all right?" whispered Leira.

Apparently, he had failed.

"No, I'm fine, it's, uh..." He should warn Brett, but how? He turned to their counselor. "Hey, Buzz, I just remembered, I left my wallet at the beach yesterday when the vog got really bad. Can I go get it?"

"All right, but don't take all day," said Buzz, who was signaling instructions to the bees with his hands. "And bring Como with you. That llama of yours needs a walk."

"Okay, thanks," said Clay, jumping up before Buzz could change his mind.

Leira watched Clay go, then looked at the wallet in her hand, puzzled. She'd lifted it from his pocket only a moment ago. There'd been no time for him to miss it.

CHAPTER
FIVE

AN ANNOUNCEMENT

There are two kinds of people in the world: people whose idea of heaven is to be stuck on a boat with nothing to do except work on their suntans and eat as much beef Wellington as they can, and people whose idea of hell it is. In other words, there are people who love cruise ships and people who hate them.

Personally, I am in the second camp. All those humans stewing together in one germ-infested pot? No, thank you! The last time I went on a cruise, there was an outbreak of stomach flu so intense that—well, you don't want to hear about that.

Naturally enough, most of the passengers on the *Imperial Conquest* were cruise lovers, or *cruisers*, as cruise-ship veterans call themselves. Inevitably, however, there were a few cruise haters aboard, who had been dragged along by their cruise-loving families. You can imagine how these disgruntled souls reacted when the ship dropped anchor without warning in the dark of night. As far as anybody could tell, they were in the middle of nowhere, and by breakfast time, anxious murmurs could be heard all over the ship. The crew tried their best to reassure worried passengers, but in truth the crew didn't know what was happening, either.

When the intercom finally beeped, signaling an announcement, everyone waited with bated breath for an explanation. Even the youngest children fell silent and listened. Only the occasional wailing baby interrupted Brett's father as he addressed the ship's passengers:

"Ladies and gentlemen, guests and crew of the *Imperial Conquest*. This is Brett Perry speaking to you from the captain's deck. Captain Abad is indisposed at the moment, but she has graciously allowed me to speak in her place.

"As the new owner of Imperial Cruise Lines, I had hoped to use this trip to introduce myself and welcome you as my friends. Sadly, tragedy has intervened. I am sorry to report there has been an accident. My only son, Brett junior, has fallen off this ship. Although I must face the fact that he may have drowned, I remain hopeful that he is still alive. In a moment, I will be leading a search party to Price

Island. That's the island you can see port side. The left side of the ship, for you landlubbers like me.* They tell me that with the direction of the ocean currents, there is a strong possibility that my son has landed there.

"In the meantime, enjoy yourselves as much as you can. The pools and spa are open. Drinks are on the house. And every passenger will receive a one-hundred-dollar chip to use in the casino. Well, every passenger over eighteen. Thank you."

Afterward, a few passengers could be heard complaining about their vacations being ruined, but even the most ardent cruise haters felt sympathy for Brett's father and agreed that he was treating them quite generously under the circumstances. They happily lined up at the casino to get their chips.

Of course, there was one person on board who

---

* THAT IS, THE LEFT SIDE WHEN FACING THE FRONT, OR BOW, OF THE SHIP, AS OPPOSED TO THE REAR, OR STERN, WHERE YOU WILL THE FIND THE DECK KNOWN AS THE POOP. (YES, I SAID POOP—WHAT OF IT?) THE RIGHT SIDE OF THE SHIP IS THE STARBOARD SIDE. IT MAY SEEM THAT THE STARBOARD SIDE SHOULD BE THE UPSIDE—IN OTHER WORDS, THE DIRECTION IN WHICH YOU ARE MOST LIKELY TO SEE STARS—BUT IN FACT THE STAR IN STARBOARD COMES NOT FROM THE NIGHT SKY BUT FROM AN OLD ENGLISH WORD FOR SNEERING. I'M SORRY, I MEANT STEERING. IT'S JUST THAT I WAS IMAGINING YOUR FACE AS YOU READ THIS FOOTNOTE. AND YOU'RE RIGHT. I'M NOT MUCH OF A SEAMAN, BUT I PROMISE I DO DO MY RESEARCH. I WOULD NEVER (WAIT FOR IT—YOU KNOW IT'S COMING) STEER YOU WRONG.

was far from happy with the announcement. She knew much of it to be untrue, and she longed to set the record straight. Unfortunately, her mouth was gagged, and she was tied to a chair in her stateroom. It is safe to say that she did not consider herself a cruise lover at the moment.

Captain Sofia Abad had lost command of her ship.

CHAPTER
SIX

FOOTPRINT

Clay was beginning to regret taking the llama with him.

"C'mon, Como," he pleaded. "*Vámonos.*"

The llama snorted disdainfully.

"I know you're not a dog. I'm sorry. *Discúlpame—*"

Como had been darting ahead of Clay for the entire hike, teasing his two-legged companion with his superior speed and agility. Now that they were finally in sight of the cave, however, the llama had decided he was done running. Como sat on his back legs like a camel, just a few feet away from the steam vent that Clay had first spotted the day before.

And when Como decided to sit, there was usually no changing his mind.

Clay sighed in frustration. Behind them, far out in the ocean, the massive cruise ship was sitting idle, like a sea monster waiting patiently for its prey. The fear in Brett's voice was still ringing in Clay's ears. He had to warn him.

"What's wrong?" Clay asked the llama. "Are you scared? *¿Tienes miedo?*"

Although Clay's Spanish was limited, he and the Peruvian camelid had a special connection, and normally they communicated with ease.* It was one of the few ways, if not the only way, in which Clay could claim an ability that might—possibly—be construed as magical. (Then again, he sometimes reminded himself, all people talked to their pets; some people even talked to their plants!) Right now, however, he had no idea what the llama was thinking. The only clue was the llama's ears. They were pointed forward—a sign of fear or danger.

"Is the volcano about to erupt? Is there a bear in the cave?** Don't tell me it's the smell—your shed smells a lot worse!"

Como's ears flattened further. Bear or no, the

---

* HAVING BEEN RAISED IN PERU, THE LLAMA, COMO C. LLAMA (WHOSE NAME, TRANSLATED FROM SPANISH, MEANS *WHAT IS YOUR NAME?*), UNDERSTANDABLY UNDERSTOOD SPANISH MUCH BETTER THAN ENGLISH. IN CASE *YOUR* ENGLISH DOES NOT EXTEND TO THE WORD *CAMELID*, THAT IS THE FAMILY OF ANIMAL TO WHICH BOTH LLAMAS AND CAMELS BELONG.
** IN FACT, THE BEAR WAS NOT SO UNLIKELY. MANY ANIMALS ROAMED FREE ON PRICE ISLAND, BEING THE DESCENDANTS OF THE FORMER INHABITANTS OF RANDOLPH PRICE'S PRIVATE ZOO. THERE WAS A FAMILY OF LEMURS LIVING NEAR CAMP, AND CLAY HAD ONCE SEEN A SMALL HERD OF ZEBRAS RUNNING ACROSS A FIELD. AS FOR PRICE, HE WAS THE DEAD BILLIONAIRE WHOSE MONEY STILL KEPT EARTH RANCH AFLOAT. CLAY HAD BEEN TOLD MANY STORIES ABOUT HIM, A FEW OF WHICH MAY EVEN HAVE BEEN TRUE.

llama was definitely afraid of something. So afraid that he seemed to have lost all capacity for language.

And he wasn't going anywhere.

"Fine, I'll go without you, but you'd better stay *aqui*, okay?—Ow!"

In his agitation, Clay had stepped too close to the steam vent. A plume of steam scalded his hand.

He blew on his hand to cool it off.

The llama's odd behavior had unnerved Clay, and he took only a tentative step into the cave before stopping.

"Hello?"

There was no bear.

There was no Brett, either.

The one thing not missing was the stench.

Clay steeled himself against the sulfur smell and took a few more steps inside.

"Brett, you in here?"

Outside, the sun was high in the sky, and the interior of the cave was brighter than it had been the day before. Clay's eyes lingered on the cave paintings, which looked even sharper and more alive upon second viewing. He could almost hear the dragons calling to one another as they flapped their wings.

He rubbed his eyes. Why did this cave make him so sleepy?

"Pee-ew! It smells worse than Kwan's sock in here!"

Clay jumped, startled.

Leira was standing inside the mouth of the cave.

"I knew you weren't looking for your wallet!" Grinning, she tossed his wallet to him. "You're so full of it."

"Thanks. Right. There it is. I should have known you'd have it." Clay glanced around nervously. Never mind his wallet; how was he going to look for Brett with Leira watching his every move?

Leira walked up beside him. "Cool drawings. So this is what you came here for—to see them?"

"Yeah, uh, I saw Flint walking out of the cave, and I decided to check it out," said Clay, more or less truthfully.

"Since when does Flint care about art?" Leira stepped closer to one of the cave paintings. "They're dinosaurs, right? What are they called—pterodactyls? It looks like those people are hunting them...."

"Well, that would be quite a discovery," said Brett, emerging out of the shadows. "Considering that the last dinosaurs died millions of years before there were any people. Or any cave paintings."

Despite looking even more bedraggled after his night in the cave, Brett held himself with great dignity—and his bow tie was still tied perfectly around his neck.

Leira stared. "*A.* You don't have to be so snotty about it. *B.* Who the heck are you?"

"That's Brett," said Clay, relieved that Brett was still alive, if a little surprised that he'd shown himself. "And those aren't dinosaurs—they're dragons."

Leira laughed. "Dragons? Dragons are supposed to be more realistic than dinosaurs?"

Clay shrugged. "All I know is they're breathing fire. Look at the red parts."

Leira scrutinized one of the drawings. "Okay, maybe that is fire. I guess that's why Flint was so into them."

She turned back to Brett and regarded him suspiciously. "That still doesn't explain your secret friend."

Clay looked at Brett. "I swear, I didn't bring her."

"You can tell her, I guess," said Brett. "Just please, both of you, don't tell anybody else I'm here."

"I'm great at keeping secrets," said Leira. "*When* I want to be."

Brett turned to Clay. "And please tell me you brought something to eat. That's the only reason I came out here."

Clay reached into his sweatshirt pocket.

Brett crossed his fingers, murmuring, "Not more trail mix, please. Not more trail mix... Wait, what is *that*—birdseed?!"

"It's a breakfast bar. And you're welcome."

"Right. Of course it is," said Brett, taking a cautious nibble. "Thanks."

"That's okay. I don't really like them, either."
Clay laughed. "Oh, here—"

He tossed Brett the bananas, mango, and flip-flops.
They landed in a pile in front of Brett's bare feet.

"Flip-flops?"

Clay gave him a look.

"Okay, okay, there's a first time for everything,
I guess." Brett eyed the shoes warily as he picked
up the bananas. You could see the dirty imprint of
Clay's toes in the rubber. "Couldn't you at least have
cleaned them first?"

Clay gave him another look.

"I know, beggars, choosers, et cetera, et cetera..."
Brett held up his hands in surrender.

"You got that right!" said Clay, amused despite
himself. Maybe Brett was annoyingly squeamish, but
at least he was funny.

As Brett tried on the flip-flops, Clay told Leira
about finding their surprise guest lying half-drowned
on the beach.

"Awesome—our very own castaway!" said Leira
when Clay finished. "So the ship that's parked out
there—that's the one you were on?"

"Oh no, it's here?" Brett grimaced as if he had a
sudden pain in his stomach. He set down the remaining banana. "I guess they're looking for me....It's
called the *Imperial Conquest*. My dad owns it."

"Wow. You must be rich." Leira smiled slyly. "I bet there's a big reward for you."

"Leira!" Clay shot her a warning look.

"Don't worry, I won't turn him in. But if you want my help, I want the whole story. Now." Leira folded her arms and looked hard at Brett. "First of all, did you really fall off? I mean, don't they have railings, and nets, and stuff? Sorry, but it's kind of hard to believe."

"Leave him alone—he almost drowned," said Clay, although he had his own suspicions.

"No, it's okay," said Brett. "She's right. I didn't exactly fall."

Leira glanced at Clay. *See.*

"You mean you jumped?" prompted Clay, who in reality was as eager to hear the story as Leira was.

"It was my dad. We had a fight...."

Brett described finding all the animals in the ship's hold, as well as the huge shipping-container-turned-cage. "There were all these guns lined up. I could tell they were planning to smuggle some kind of big, scary animal—like a lion or a tiger, maybe, but, I don't know...bigger. At least, that's what it looked like. And the live animals were there for it to eat, I think."

"All that to smuggle one animal?" said Clay, dubious.

"Are you kidding? There's a huge black market," said Brett. "Haven't you heard about the rhinos? They're practically extinct now because of their horns."

Leira nodded knowingly. "It's like shark fins. People are crazy. They think eating them will cure all their illnesses."*

Clay looked at her skeptically.

"What, it's called the Internet," she said, brushing him off.

"She's right," said Brett. "And don't forget elephants. My dad went on this secret elephant hunt once. It's disgusting."

"Tell me about it," said Leira, who considered

---

* ARE YOU SUPERSTITIOUS? I'M NOT. WELL, NOT VERY. SO MAYBE I HAVE TO WEAR THE SAME PAIR OF PURPLE POLKA-DOT BOXERS WHENEVER I SIT DOWN TO A GAME OF DOMINOES. THEY BRING ME LUCK. SOMETIMES. AND I PROMISE, I DO WASH THEM. OCCASIONALLY. THE QUESTION IS, AM I HURTING ANYONE? ANSWER: NO.

OTHER SUPERSTITIONS, I'M AFRAID, ARE NOT SO HARMLESS. TAKE BRETT'S EXAMPLE: THE RHINOCEROS. IN ASIAN COUNTRIES, MANY PEOPLE BELIEVE THAT A RHINO HORN HAS MAGICAL HEALING POWERS. AS A RESULT, A SINGLE HORN SELLS FOR AS MUCH AS A MILLION DOLLARS, AND THE ENTIRE RHINO POPULATION IS BEING HUNTED TO EXTINCTION. AND IT'S NOT JUST RHINOS. SHARK FINS. TIGER BONES. WHALE FECES. (YES, I MEAN WHALE POOP. AKA AMBERGRIS. ASK ME ABOUT IT SOME OTHER TIME.) ALL HAVE BEEN SOUGHT FOR THEIR SUPPOSED MAGICAL POWERS. IT MATTERS NOT THAT THESE POWERS AREN'T REAL; PEOPLE PAY ANYWAY. OF COURSE, AN ANIMAL WOULD HAVE TO BE VERY VALUABLE INDEED—MANY TIMES MORE VALUABLE THAN A RHINOCEROS—TO MAKE IT WORTH COMMANDEERING A CRUISE SHIP.

herself a dedicated animal rights activist. "The ivory trade. Circuses. Elephants are abused everywhere."

Brett nodded. "Anyway, it was obvious my dad was doing something horrible, and probably illegal. Operation St. George, they called it—"

"St. George? Why?" asked Clay.

Brett shrugged. "I don't know. It was like a code name or something."

"Don't interrupt, Clay." Leira turned to Brett. "So—?"

"So when he caught me in that cage, at first I didn't say anything, but when he started yelling at me for spying, something just snapped, and I told him that he was disgusting and evil and I hated him and I hoped whatever animal he was hunting ate him for dinner. I know, really mature..." Brett rolled his eyes. "Then I ran out, and he chased me all the way onto the deck, yelling that he'll teach me not to talk to him like that and whatever....And when he caught me, he grabbed me so hard I screamed that I was going to report him to Child Services. And that I was going to call Greenpeace or PETA about his animal-hunting operation. I didn't even know what I was saying. It was crazy, but I guess my dad believed me, because he went totally ballistic. He started shaking me harder and harder, saying, 'You'll never be a real man, you're no son of mine, I never want to see you again'—et cetera, et cetera. He sounded like a dad in some old movie...." Brett tried to roll his eyes again, but it was apparent that he was forcing back tears.

"Anyway, I told him to let go of me, and maybe I hit him—I can't really even remember—and the captain of the ship, she tried to stop him, but she couldn't, and—well, I don't know if he really meant to, or if he just pushed too hard, but..." Brett trailed off.

"He pushed you off the boat? His own son? He could have killed you!" Leira exclaimed. "Sorry, I didn't mean to sound so excited...."

"Now you see why I don't want my dad to find me?" A tear trickled down Brett's face.

He hastily wiped it away, and Clay and Leira pretended not to notice. They had had their own troubles with their parents, but nothing like this. It was unimaginable.

"So what's your plan?" asked Leira finally. "Just hide here until the ship leaves?"

Brett wiped his eyes. "I guess."

"Okay," said Leira. "Then what?"

"The seaplane comes tomorrow to deliver supplies," said Clay, glancing at her. "I was thinking we could try to stow him away on it."

"I don't know. That plane lands all the way on the other side of the island," said Leira, skeptical. "And it's pretty small."

"It doesn't matter," said Brett eagerly. "You can

pack me in a box and tie it up with string. Anything's better than seeing my dad again."

"All right, if that's what you want, we'll figure it out," said Leira, despite her misgivings. "It'll be good practice. You never know when you're going to have to plan a quick getaway, right?"

Brett smiled. "Great. I'll see you tomorrow, then?"

They nodded

"I'll come back tonight," said Clay. "And maybe bring you something better than birdseed if I can scrounge it up."

"That would be fantastic," said Brett. "But only if it's, you know, not too much trouble."

Clay laughed. "Oh, it's trouble, all right, but whatever...." He shrugged.

"Seriously," said Brett, looking him in the eye. "Thanks. Nobody's ever helped me out like this. It's really...cool of you. Both of you. Not that I've ever been stranded on a desert island before, but—you know what I mean."

"Shut up," said Clay, reddening. "Now you're embarrassing me."

"Don't say 'shut up,'" admonished Leira. "It's rude."

Brett laughed. "Hey, I almost forgot. Look what I found—"

He held up a disk-shaped rock imprinted with what looked like three reptilian toes. "I know I was the one knocking the dinosaur theory, but doesn't it look like one of those fossilized dinosaur footprints—you know, like you see at a natural history museum?"

"Nah. If you listened to Clay here, you'd know it's obviously a dragon print," Leira joked. "You can tell by the shape of the toenails. Like little daggers."

"Heh." Clay forced a laugh.

He was starting to feel that strange sleepiness again, and for some reason he didn't think her joke was very funny.

They found Como sitting where Clay had left him, his ears still pointed forward. If anything, the llama looked more frightened of the cave than he had before.

"Hey, you don't think, in that cave, there couldn't be—there couldn't ever have really been—" Clay stammered to Leira. "I mean, those are just paintings, right? Never mind. I'm being dumb."

"You said it, not me." Leira smirked.

"Thanks for the encouragement."

"Seriously," said Leira, lowering her voice, "the only thing in there you need to worry about is Brett. What if he finds out about camp?"

"You mean about the magic?" said Clay, lowering his voice as well, even though they were well out of Brett's hearing range.

"Yes, I mean the magic, duh. If he tells any outsiders, it'll be all over the news in seconds, and this

place will be swarming. Everybody at camp will want to kill us. *I* will want to kill us."

"Don't worry, he's not going to find out," said Clay, with more confidence than he felt.

Leira looked sideways at him. "Are you sure we shouldn't tell Mr. B about him? Just in case."

"Yes, I'm sure. . . . C'mon, Como, let's go home."

He gave the llama a pat on the head, uncertain whether he was trying to reassure Como or himself.

From Secrets of the Occulta Draco; or, The Memoirs of a Dragon Tamer

Lesson the first:

Always remember, dear apprentice Dragon Tamer, that you are not and never will be a tamer of dragons. A dragon is not a lion in a circus. A dragon cannot be tamed any more than it can be caged. It is foolish to think so—and almost certain death if you try.

As a man knowledgeable in the ways of dragons once said, "Wiser it is to kill a dragon than to chain it. For a dragon is the very essence of wildness and will not stay chained for long."

Nonetheless, it is as Dragon Tamers that our kind has always been known; and it is as Dragon Tamers that history shall remember us, if it remembers us at all.

What does a Dragon Tamer do with a dragon if not tame it? The short answer is, nothing.

This is much more difficult than it sounds. There are very few people who have the strength to do nothing in the presence of a dragon.

Dragons, through no fault of their own, arouse great passions in our excitable little species. When meeting a dragon, most humans are overcome by terror; and if not terror, they are overwhelmed by greed or anger or pride or jealousy. If they are not convinced that their world is about to end, then they are convinced that great power and wealth are within their grasp; and they are willing to take great risks to attain those things.

Dragon-frenzy, we call it.

A Dragon Tamer, on the other hand, does not react to a dragon except as one being to another. Yes, after he (or she! Some of the best Tamers I have known are women) has been with a dragon a great while, he may stroke its neck, or clean its scales, or sharpen its claws. He may roast a leg of mutton with the dragon's breath. (Only, of course, after the dragon has eaten first!) A Dragon Tamer may even, in certain unusual circumstances, fly on the dragon's back. But first and foremost, the Tamer shows that he desires nothing for himself other than to share the air the dragon breathes and the earth the dragon treads.

There are only three rules when it comes to dragons. We call them the Three Precepts.

I. Ask naught from a dragon but to share the air around you.
II. Deny naught that a dragon asks for but the soul within you.
III. Refuse naught that a dragon offers but to breathe upon you.

CHAPTER
SEVEN

SOS

Despite what you may have heard, *SOS* does not stand for *Save Our Ship*. The famous three-letter distress signal came into being only because it is so simple to reproduce in Morse code.* It might just as easily stand for *Sink Our Sailboat* or *Seize Our Submarine*. Or, for that matter, *Spill Our Soup* or *Steal Our Sandwich*.

For the campers and counselors of Earth Ranch, *SOS* was not a distress signal at all; instead, the letters stood for the name of a certain society to which they all belonged: a secret society, the Society of the Other Side.

Nonetheless, when the bees stopped Leira and

---

* No doubt you already know how to represent the letters *SOS* in Morse code. However, it bears repeating just in case: ••• – – – ••• (three short beeps, three long, three short). You never know when the need for a distress signal might arise.

Clay on their way back to camp and flew into SOS formation, the two young society members knew the message must be urgent. Sure enough, a moment later, the bees regrouped to form the initials **PPL** followed by the number **12**. Clay and Leira understood immediately: There would be an emergency society meeting at the Price Public Library at noon—the first such meeting that had been held that summer.

A round stone tower that looked like it could have been built in the Middle Ages, the Price Public Library was in reality fewer than a hundred years old. Still, it was one of the oldest structures on Price Island (not that there were many to choose from), and by far the biggest to have survived the volcanic explosion that left Randolph Price's mansion, Price Palace, in ruins.

When Clay and Leira (and the llama) arrived a few minutes early for the SOS meeting, a tattered canvas teepee was incongruously tethered to a post in front of the library. Although there was no wind, the teepee appeared to be straining to get free and fly away like a kite. They watched it with curiosity, the llama especially. (What sort of animal is this, he must have wondered.) It was unusual to see Mr. Bailey's summer residence up close; most often, the skittish teepee hid in the vog, away from the prying eyes of young campers.

Leira's sister, Mira, was standing by the library

door. As always when he saw them together, Clay marveled that two people could resemble each other so much and so little at the same time. Leira, the vegan thief, in her newsboy hat and suspenders; Mira, the bookish actress, with her long hair and summer dress (an unusual choice at Earth Ranch, where everyone else wore jeans)—their styles couldn't have been more different. And yet their faces and their coloring were so similar that anybody who looked at all closely could see they were sisters.

Mira watched Clay tie Como to the post, next to the teepee.

"You guys are the first ones here. Except for Mr. B—" She tilted her head, indicating his teepee. "I'm supposed to guard the door."

Leira wrinkled her face. "Since when does anybody guard anything on this island?"

"Since some strange speedboat landed on the beach, I guess," said Mira. "Did you see it?"

"Landed? Did it come from the cruise ship?" asked Clay, feeling a creeping sense of dread.

"Think so. Buzz went down to check it out. Did you find your wallet?"

"Yep. Right where I left it." Clay avoided Mira's eyes. He wasn't nearly as talented an actor as she was.

"Oh, good." Mira smiled at Leira in a way that was more like a frown. "I made a bet that my sister had taken it again."

Leira smiled back—in the same unsmiling way. "Not this time."

"So why'd you go after him, then?" said Mira, clearly disbelieving. "You just thought you'd give him a helping hand?"

"Uh-huh."

A look passed between Leira and Mira. Actually, several looks. They were not always the best of friends, but they regularly held long conversations without saying a word.

Clay had no idea what the tension between them was about; he only knew he wanted to stay out of it. He focused instead on the crumbling building in front of them.

Weeks earlier, when Clay had first discovered the old library tower, he'd imagined that it was haunted by ghosts of the dead. As it turned out, he wasn't far off. At least, there were hardly any *living* souls inside. A public library in name only, the Price Public Library had never officially opened while Randolph Price was alive. Nowadays, it was open to Earth Ranch campers, but only on special occasions. The secretive billionaire's copious collections of rare books and *objets* had to be handled very carefully; indeed, many things in the library were never to be handled at all.*

---

* IN FRENCH, *OBJETS* MEANS "OBJECTS" (AS IN "THINGS," NOT AS IN "MAKING AN OBJECTION"), AND TO BE HONEST, THERE WASN'T MUCH REASON FOR ME NOT TO WRITE *OBJECT* IN THE FIRST PLACE. BUT I THINK

Today, entering the library with Leira, Clay felt again as though he were stepping not backward in time so much as into a place where time had stopped. Or where all times occurred at once. Partly it was the way sunlight filtered down through the dusty air from the large round skylight. Partly it was the way the long, sloping balcony spiraled down from the top of the tower all the way to the bottom floor, several stories underground. Whichever way you looked, the library seemed to spin slowly in one direction or the other.

It was disorienting and compelling at the same time.

"I swear, someday I'm coming back here with my skateboard," he said.

Leira scoffed. "Yeah, you wish."

"Come out, come out, wherever you are!"

They'd expected to find Mr. Bailey busy preparing for the SOS meeting. Instead, they found their camp's director crawling on all fours underneath the big old banyan tree that grew out of the library's stone floor.

"Where are you, my little friend?" Mr. Bailey called, his voice ringing throughout the library. (He had spent many years in the theater and always

---

YOU'LL AGREE THAT THE FRENCH WORD HAS A CERTAIN *JE NE SAIS QUOI* THAT THE ENGLISH WORD LACKS.

83

sounded like he was addressing the back row.) "I know you're here somewhere!"

Long, dangling roots slapped him on his butt as he crawled around the tree. Clay stifled a laugh.

"Uh, hi, Mr. B," said Leira bravely. "What are you looking for? Can we help?"

"Oh, hello! I didn't see you—"

Mr. Bailey stood up and stepped out from under the tree, seemingly unembarrassed to have been caught in such an undignified pose.

"Did Harry sneak in again?" asked Leira.

Harry was the camp cat. The last time he got into the library, he'd been locked inside for weeks.

"Ah, if only." Mr. Bailey sighed. "I'm afraid it's a little more serious than that. A book is missing."

"You were talking to a book?" asked Clay, unable to hide his surprise.

"Well, not just any book—one of our underground residents."

Mr. Bailey nodded to an open hatch door at the base of the banyan tree.

As Clay well remembered, though he had only been through it once, the door led to a secret chamber known simply as the Tree Room. The Tree Room was a library-within-the-library, a magic library, where Randolph Price had installed his prize collection of grimoires—those magical books in which you might find the recipe for a potion that turns your brother green or instructions for bewitching your math teacher. Alas, campers were seldom allowed to look at the grimoires, let alone remove one.

"You think somebody stole it?" asked Leira, whose mind always went to theft even when she wasn't contemplating stealing anything herself.

"Oh no," said Mr. Bailey, appalled. "I trust everyone at this camp implicitly."

"What then?" said Leira. She was not nearly so trusting herself.

"It must have escaped. Sometimes they do when the door isn't shut properly. In fact—" Mr. Bailey lunged for the open hatch door, where a few old leather books could be seen fluttering around. (The magic in the grimoires was such that sometimes the Tree Room resembled an aviary more than a library.) "Oh no, you don't!" He slammed the door shut before another literary inmate could escape.

"I only hope it hasn't flown too far," he said. "Today is not a good day to have a grimoire on the loose! What with strange boats landing on the island...Which reminds me..."

Mr. Bailey checked his ornate and oversized pocket watch, the only one Clay had ever seen with minute and second hands that looked and moved like actual hands. At the moment, the minute hand was making a number one while the second hand was making circles with its pointer finger, indicating that it was time to get a move on.

"Patience!" Mr. Bailey scolded his watch. "I know we have another two minutes at least."

"So what book was it?" asked Clay, dreading the answer.

Secrets of the Occulta Draco was still sitting at the bottom of his backpack. Maybe it was Flint who had stolen it from the library, but Clay knew if he didn't return it soon, he was no better than a thief himself.

"A book about dragons," said Mr. Bailey. "One of a kind, absolutely irreplaceable."

"Dragons?" Clay repeated, his mouth dry.

"That's funny," said Leira, eyeing Clay. "We were just talking about dragons."

Clay's leg started to jiggle with anxiety. Was it his imagination, or was the book standing up inside his backpack, as if it were listening to their conversation?

"So this book—it has some kind of dragon magic?" Clay asked, trying to sound as casual as possible. "Like, how to put spells on dragons or something?"

"I'm ashamed to say I've never read it," said Mr. Bailey. "But, yes, that's my understanding. Supposedly it was written by a famous Dragon Master."

You mean Tamer, Clay almost corrected but stopped himself just in time.

The night before, he had stayed up late reading,

imagining himself a Dragon Tamer from centuries past, but he hadn't paid much attention to any references to magic or spells. He just assumed that the book was fiction, a make-believe memoir. If it was an actual grimoire, there was no telling what kind of powers the book might have.

Leira frowned. "Wait, back up. Does that mean you think dragons are real?...Or were?"

"Who knows," said Mr. Bailey. "But why would there be so many stories about them, in so many different cultures, if they never existed?" He raised an eyebrow, as if daring the campers to contradict him.

"As a matter of fact, the builder of this library, Randolph Price, believed there were once dragons on this very island."

"Dragons...here?" Clay felt a prickling sensation in his neck. He tried not to look at Leira.

"Why not? One imagines they might like volcanoes." Mr. Bailey smiled. It was hard to tell how serious he was. "A thousand years ago, a group of Pacific Islanders landed here—we know this from archaeological evidence. Why did they not survive? Randolph's theory was that they tried to hunt the dragons, and in return the dragons hunted them." He waved his hand, as if to indicate a dragon picking off the islanders in one fell swoop.

Mr. B checked his watch again. The second hand was going berserk. "Now it's really time for our meeting, but later, if you're interested, there's a shelf full of dragon lore upstairs. Under the painting of St. George and the dragon."

"St. George?" Clay echoed, his head spinning. That was the name of Brett's father's "operation."

"Surely you know the story of St. George," said Mr. Bailey. "The first knight to slay a dragon for a princess...?"*

The bottom floor of the library had filled up while they were speaking. Most people seemed to be thinking about the meeting ahead, but a few looked at Clay and Leira with open curiosity. Clay could tell that

---

* A BRIEF HISTORY OF DRAGON-SLAYING:

ACCORDING TO MEDIEVAL MYTH, THERE WAS ONCE A FEARSOME DRAGON THAT TERRORIZED A TOWN FOR MANY YEARS. EVERY SO OFTEN, ONE CHILD FROM THE TOWN WAS CHOSEN AT RANDOM AS A SACRIFICE TO THE DRAGON'S VORACIOUS APPETITE. NO ONE WAS SAFE FROM THIS HORRIBLE LOTTERY, OR HUNGER GAME, IF YOU WILL, INCLUDING THE DAUGHTER OF THE KING. BUT JUST WHEN SHE WAS SLOTTED TO BE THE DRAGON'S NEXT DINNER, THE PROVERBIAL KNIGHT IN SHINING ARMOR, ST. GEORGE, ARRIVED ON A WHITE HORSE, PROMISING TO SLAY THE DRAGON, AND SLAY THE DRAGON HE DID. AFTERWARD, HE CLAIMED THE PRINCESS AS HIS WIFE—A FATE PRESUMABLY LESS ONEROUS FOR THE PRINCESS THAN BEING EATEN, BUT WHO KNOWS.... ST. GEORGE APPEARS IN MANY PLACES IN THE HISTORY OF ART AND LITERATURE, PERHAPS MOST FAMOUSLY IN THE EPIC POEM OF WIZARDS AND DRAGONS CALLED THE FAERIE QUEENE. DESPITE WHAT MR. BAILEY SUGGESTS, HOWEVER, ST. GEORGE IS NOT NECESSARILY THE FIRST TO HAVE SLAYED A DRAGON FOR A PRINCESS. LONG BEFORE THERE WERE STORIES ABOUT ST. GEORGE, THERE WAS THE MYTH OF ANDROMEDA, A PRINCESS WHO WAS CHAINED TO A ROCK AND SACRIFICED TO THE SEA MONSTER CETUS—ONLY TO BE SAVED BY THE ORIGINAL GREEK HERO, PERSEUS. PERSEUS, IT SEEMS, HAD A TALENT FOR MONSTER-SLAYING. HE WAS ALSO THE ONE TO BEHEAD THE SNAKE-HAIRED GORGON, MEDUSA. TAKE THAT, ST. GEORGE.

Mira was especially interested in what they'd been talking about. Leira, of course, gave away nothing. She just looked blankly back at her sister.

Buzz was the last to arrive. As soon as Buzz entered, Mr. Bailey asked the campers to quiet down, then turned back to the beekeeper. "Well, what news have you? Is it a search party?"

Buzz nodded gravely. "Yes. A boy fell off the boat, and they say currents may have swept him here. I offered the camp's assistance."

"Good," said Mr. Bailey.

"Every minute counts," said Buzz. "If the boy was lucky enough to make it ashore alive, he is probably very weak and dehydrated. He may be unconscious."

Or just in a really bad mood, Clay thought.

Mr. Bailey nodded vigorously. "We must all help with the search! But please, friends," he said, addressing the campers, "no funny stuff. I know, in an emergency like this, the rule might seem trivial, but the likelihood that magic will help us find the boy is slim. And the risk of outsiders discovering the true nature of this place— it's too great. There are certain books here that if people knew they existed . . . well, they would stop at nothing to get them. And the consequences! It's not just that they would wreak havoc with love potions, or even that sudden piles of gold would upend the economy. Think of the mass hysteria when the public learned not only that Isaac Newton was a practicing alchemist but that the laws of physics are subject to other laws entirely! And then there are those craven people—monsters I should say, not people—who already know of magic but misunderstand its meaning. If they were to find this library . . ." He shuddered at the thought. "I'm sorry to go on at such length, but I hope I make myself understood."

Mr. Bailey scanned the crowd for nodding heads. They all knew which books he was referring to: the grimoires. But only Clay and Leira knew that he was thinking of one in particular.

"Good," said Mr. Bailey. "Now, I have a feeling some of you are better acquainted with this island's hiding spots than I am—don't ask me why."

The campers tittered. There was an invisible Wall of Trust that surrounded the camp, which campers were not supposed to cross without permission. Eventually, however, most ventured out into the island wilderness at one time or another—only to find themselves playing a game of hide-and-seek with the bees.

Mr. Bailey smiled. "It seems you know what I'm talking about. So, does anyone have an idea where to look? Somewhere the boy might have gone, seeking water or shelter? A spring in the bamboo forest? A cave among the rocks?"

Squirming, Clay did his best to avoid looking at Mr. Bailey. Between the book in his backpack and the boy in the cave, he was beginning to feel downright deceitful.

Inadvertently, Clay's eyes landed on Flint, who had slipped into the meeting after it started. Flint was biting his lip, and Clay could see that he was thinking of the cave, too.

"Don't worry, he's not going to say anything," Leira whispered in Clay's ear. "Flint doesn't care about some boy he's never met; he only cares about himself."

She was right. Flint didn't say a word as Mr. Bailey finished talking, and a moment later the campers were being divided into search teams. All teams were to return to the library in an hour's time.

While everyone else poured out of the library, Clay pulled Leira upstairs.

It took them a few moments to locate the painting because it was very small—not much more than a foot wide—and very dark, with swirling gray smoke covering most of the canvas. But when they looked closely, the dragon was unmistakable, deep red and scaly, with a twisting tail and sharp talons.

Above the dragon, a knight in shining armor—St. George—sat astride a rearing white horse. The knight held a long spear that drove straight into the dragon's mouth and out the back of his neck, making blood spurt in all directions. A gruesome image.

Clay stared. "That is..." He shook his head, his eyes focused on all the blood.

"Gross?" finished Leira.

In the background, a beautiful woman in a gauzy dress—the princess—was chained to the front of a rocky cave. Clay could tell he was supposed to feel grateful that the knight was protecting her. And yet there was something about the dragon's eyes—the way they showed pain and anger and pride all at once—that made Clay sympathize more with the fearsome beast than with the demure princess.

At the bottom of the painting was a brass plaque:

St. George Fighting the Dragon, circa 1610
(painter unknown)

"I thought knights were supposed to be the good guys..." Clay muttered.

"Yeah, right." Leira laughed. "So were cowboys, but ask the Native Americans how they felt."

"I'm serious. It's messed up that we're supposed to think he's a hero."

"C'mon," said Leira, already walking away. "If we don't get going, somebody else is going to find Brett before we do. Then we'll all be in trouble."

"Okay, okay," said Clay, studying the shelf in front of him. It was full of books about dragons—from the dragons of Arthurian legend to the dragons painted on Chinese vases. He had planned to slip *Secrets of the Occulta Draco* in among them, to avoid having to give the book directly to Mr. B, but now

that he was here, the plan seemed to make less sense. What if Mr. B never found the book and it just stayed there forever? Or, worse, what if it flew away?

Besides, he wasn't done reading it.

As he hurried to catch up with Leira, he glanced back at the painting of St. George. He felt almost as though the dragon were looking at him, beseeching him for help.

CHAPTER
EIGHT

MISSING

Even if Flint hadn't told anyone about the cave, it was no longer a safe place for Brett to lie low; there was too much of a chance that he would be discovered by somebody from camp—or, worse, somebody from the ship. Clay and Leira knew they had to warn him, but how to get back to the cave without anyone seeing them?

As soon as they left the library, they were accosted by Mira.

"Oh, so cute," she teased. "Look at the little search buddies. You better hold hands so you don't lose each other."

Leira looked like she wanted to retaliate, and for a second Clay feared they would break into an all-out fight. Instead, Leira ignored her sister and pushed ahead without looking at her—or Clay.

"Whatever." Mira sniffed and turned back to join her own teammates.

The other Worms—a team of three—walked up to Clay, grins on their faces.

"You got your hands full with the ladies, huh?" said Kwan.

Clay shrugged. "Yeah. What's up with them? They've been like that for days. I keep getting caught in the cross fire."

Pablo laughed. "What's up with them? Like you don't know."

Clay stopped walking, confused. "What do you mean?"

"Seriously, you don't know what they're fighting over?" said Jonah.

"No..."

Jonah flicked Clay in the chest. "You, you doofus."

"Really? Why?"

"Because they like you. Duh." Jonah grinned evilly.

"Yeah. It's obvious," said Kwan. "You're the only one who doesn't see it."

Clay looked like he was going to be sick. "No way, not possible..."

There'd been gossip about him and Leira before, but he always discounted it; they were like squabbling siblings, nothing like girlfriend and boyfriend.

And Mira was Leira's actual squabbling sibling. So Clay and Mira were squabbling siblings by default.

And there was a difference between *liking* and *liking to squabble*, Clay told himself. Wasn't there?

Pablo pointed ahead to Leira, who was beckoning for Clay. "Look—Girlfriend Number One wants you now."

"Seriously, you guys don't know what you're talking about."

The last thing Clay wanted to do at that moment was go anywhere with Leira, but he had no choice. Blushing red and feeling like the whole camp was watching him, he ran ahead to join her.

They were so concerned with staying out of sight of the other kids from camp that they almost didn't see the three strangers patrolling Bamboo Bay. Just as Clay was about to step out onto the sand—and straight into the patrol—Leira tugged on his arm and dragged him behind a clump of bamboo.

Unfortunately, there was no way to get to the cave without walking on the beach. They were stuck.

"This way!" shouted a voice.

Brushing the leaves out of their eyes, the nervous campers watched the island's new intruders march past, not more than five feet away. With their black uniforms and assault rifles, they looked more like a

SWAT team hunting for a terrorist than like sailors searching for a missing boy.

"What do they think—that Brett is going to blow up the island?" Clay murmured.

"Maybe they're afraid of cannibals," Leira joked in a whisper.

"Maybe. Or maybe they're not looking for Brett at all."

"What do you mean? What else would they be doing?"

"Nothing. I didn't mean anything," said Clay, unwilling to voice his real suspicion.

They had to wait several minutes before the path was clear. Even then, they could see the rifles gleaming in the distance; venturing out into the open still seemed like a risky move.

"Don't run," warned Leira. "If they see us, we're just looking for Brett, like all the other kids."

Clay nodded, and they began to walk quietly across the sand.

One man turned back toward them, shading his eyes with one hand. Clay and Leira dove into the beckoning bank of bamboo trees, not a moment too soon.

"He's just looking at the volcano," Leira said. She didn't sound completely convinced, though, and they were both relieved when the man turned back around to join the others.

Clay and Leira made it the rest of the way without encountering anyone else, armed or unarmed, but when they got to the cave, they were greeted by an unwelcome sight—something almost worse than running into another patrolman.

Flint.

He was talking into a phone and seemed even more startled to see them than they were to see him.

Casually, he slipped the phone into his pocket, but it was too late. They'd seen it, and he knew it. Of all the rules at Earth Ranch, the no-technology rule was one of the most serious. *No screen, no phone—or you go home.*

"What are you guys doing here?" he demanded, but the words didn't come out with his usual cockiness. It was the first time Clay could remember Flint sounding flustered.

"We're looking for the boy—duh." Leira looked him up and down. "What are *you* doing?"

"Same," said Flint. "He's not here. Turn around. Everybody's supposed to be back in fifteen minutes anyway."

Clay and Leira glanced at each other. Was Flint telling the truth?

Clay pointed to the cave entrance. "What's in there?" He tried to look like he didn't know, which mostly meant scrunching up his nose and squinting as if he were trying to see something.

"Nothing." Flint shrugged.

"Looks like a cave," said Clay. "Can we look inside?"

Flint stared hard at him. Apparently, Clay's act wasn't very convincing. "It was you, wasn't it? You took the book. I should have known.... Give it back. Now."

"What book?" Clay could feel his leg starting to jiggle with anxiety. "I don't know what you're talking about."

Flint laughed, his confidence restored. "Sure you don't. Then where were you after Capture the Flag?"

"Nowhere. Lost."

"Yeah?" Flint's eyes glinted dangerously. "Come here and say that to my face, Worm."

"Funny, speaking of faces," said Leira, stepping between them. "Or not really faces, but heads. Or, like, the ears on them..."

Flint looked at her like she was insane. "You know you're talking out loud, right?"

Leira patted her pocket. "That thing in your pocket, it looked like a phone...."

"It's a satellite phone," said Flint quickly. "It's the camp's—not that it's any of your freaking business."

"Oh, so it's no big deal if I ask Mr. B about it?" said Leira.

Glaring, Flint clenched his fists so hard that sparks started to fly out of them. Clay feared he would start throwing fireballs—which actually would have been pretty cool, as long as they didn't happen to land on Clay or Leira.

Leira smiled, almost but not quite sweetly. She knew she had won, at least this round. "Mind if we go look in the cave now?"

Finally, Flint unclenched his fists. "Fine, but be quick. And don't even think of telling anyone what's in there. If you do, I'll know—"

"Thanks," said Leira cheerily, although Clay could tell she too had been scared. A person really had to try hard to seem that composed. Especially when Flint was involved.

"By the way, that bamboo stick by your feet— were you using it as a torch?" asked Leira. "Will you light it for us?"

Flint gave her a look—she was pressing her luck— but he lit the stick on fire with a snap of his fingers.

"Don't burn yourself," he sneered, handing it to her.

Without another word, he brushed past them and headed down to the beach.

"That's not the camp's phone," said Leira, watching him go. "Wonder where he got it."

"I wonder who he was talking to," said Clay.

Leira snickered. "Probably some girl."

"I don't know. It looked kind of serious."

"Yeah, I guess. You don't know what book he

meant, do you?" She looked at Clay. "Or why he thought you had it?"

Clay shook his head, avoiding her eyes. "Beats me."

They waited in the cave for about five minutes, calling Brett's name intermittently.

"Maybe he saw Flint coming and found a new hiding place," said Leira.

"You don't think his dad's guys got him, do you?" said Clay.

Leira shook her head. "Think about it: If they'd found him, why would they still be searching the beach?"

"Yeah, unless—"

"What?"

"I just have a weird feeling, that's all." Clay looked at one of the dragon drawings on the wall. "It's probably crazy."

Leira followed his eyes. "Okay, I *think* I know what you're thinking. But just because it's called Operation St. George doesn't mean they're here to slay a dragon—"

"Capture a dragon, then," said Clay, relieved finally to be discussing it aloud.

"Whatever. First of all, who really believes in dragons?" said Leira. "I mean, besides Mr. B. *And* believes in them enough to hijack a gazillion-dollar cruise ship?"

"What about that footprint Brett found? Isn't that proof...of something?" Clay couldn't bring himself to say that it was a dream that was making him think the unthinkable.

"Second of all, what about Brett?" said Leira, ignoring him. "Are you saying it's just a coincidence that he got pushed off the ship and swam to the exact island where they happened to be coming to hunt dragons? That's pretty unlikely, unless..." Leira faltered.

"Unless what?"

"Well, unless it was some sort of setup," said Leira hesitantly.

Clay looked at her in surprise. "You think Brett is in on it?"

"I didn't say that! I'm not the one who thinks they're hunting dragons. All I'm saying is that if they were..."

"A missing kid would be a good excuse?"

Leira nodded.

"So maybe that's why his dad pushed him," said Clay. "It doesn't mean Brett knew about it."

"Maybe, maybe not," said Leira. "You have to admit that his story was a little out there.... Either way, it's time to tell Mr. B."

"But we promised—"

"I know, but what if somebody from camp finds Brett? We don't want them just to deliver him to the ship. I mean, if he's *not* in on it...Forget about dragons—those guys have guns!"

She had a point.

"All right," said Clay reluctantly. "You go find Mr. B. I'll stay here a little longer. In case Brett comes back."

Leira nodded solemnly and held out the flaming bamboo stick.

After she left, Clay paced back and forth, fretting. *Was* it possible Brett had been in on his father's plans all along? Brett could be irritating, sure—very irritating—and the whole bow tie thing was a little weird, but he didn't seem like a liar...or a dragon thief. Clay considered himself a good judge of character. Then again, he'd fallen for simple tricks before. Take that game of Capture the Flag, for instance. Maybe he was just a gullible guy.

To give himself something to do, he walked the perimeter of the cave, bamboo torch held high, examining the darker recesses more closely than he had before. Most of the paintings were near the cave entrance, but on his second circuit Clay noticed a peculiar symbol—three red lines joined at the bottom—painted on the wall.

"What the—" He reached out to touch the rough

stone, and a dot of red pigment flaked off onto his finger.

The symbol looked like a downward-pointing arrow—or maybe an upside-down volcano?—and he looked at his feet to see if it was directing him to something on the ground. He didn't see anything except rock and sand. However, when he looked up, he noticed an identical symbol about three feet away. And then another and another.

They were markers, or road signs, painted at regular intervals, directing him deeper into the mountain.

The cave was about fifty feet long and descended so steeply toward the back that he had to dig his toes into the ground to slow down. The symbols continued almost the entire way, then stopped, for no apparent reason, before the cave ended. Clay held the torch close to the wall where the next symbol should have been, but he didn't see even a trace of paint.

The cave trail had gone cold. Maybe the markers had been directing him toward something that was no longer there.

Just as he was about to turn around, Clay stepped on something squishy, and his foot slid a few inches.

Ick.

What had he stepped on? Bear poop? A frog?

He looked down and laughed; it was a banana peel, and he'd almost slipped on it, like in an old cartoon. No doubt Brett had left it there.

What a slob, Clay thought.

And then he thought, Wait a second....

A slob was the one thing Brett wasn't.

What had made such a fastidious guy drop a banana peel on the ground like that?

Why had Brett come down all this way, and where had he gone?

Clay shivered. It struck him that he was totally, utterly alone. If something should happen to him, he might never be found. That is, unless somebody else followed the trail of red symbols.

Moving his torch around, he examined the area around him once more. This time he saw it:

Near the banana peel, there was another red symbol painted on a rock—but this one much larger and much closer to the ground than the others. Next to the symbol, half-covered under a layer of sand, was a fossilized footprint like the one Brett had shown Clay and Leira earlier, although this one was even bigger and seemed to be embedded in solid rock.

Clay moved his torch closer and looked from the

footprint to the three intersecting red lines painted next to it. Then he thought about the painted creatures on the upper cave walls, the ones with the tongues that were not tongues but flames.

The red lines were a symbol, all right, but only now did he understand what they represented: not an arrow or a volcano but a footprint.

And not just any footprint.

A *dragon* footprint.

His mind reeling with the implications, Clay put his own foot where, a millennium ago, the dragon—if it had really been a dragon—had put its foot. The footprint was so big Clay could almost have sat down inside it. He could only imagine how large a beast would make such a footprint.

As Clay's weight bore down on it, the rock in which the footprint was embedded began to sink, like a giant stone button. There was a groaning sound and the screech of rock scraping against rock.

Above him, the cave wall was moving.

Most Dragon Tamers feel deep empathy for animals of all kinds. Long before meeting a dragon, the future Tamer will likely have had a special connection not just with a cat or a dog or a horse, but with a wilder animal as well. An owl, perhaps, or a deer or a bear. This person and this animal—it will have felt as though they were speaking to each other. In fact, they *were* speaking to each other in the ways that count most.

Alas, dragons themselves do not have much empathy for other animals. It is well known, for example, that dragons don't like cats. Tradition has it that this is because dragons are related to birds, however distantly. I have another interpretation. I think dragons don't like cats because cats remind dragons of themselves. Like cats, dragons are inscrutable creatures, indifferent to others, and their predominant trait is laziness. A dragon's preferred activity at any given moment is to lie in the sun, and if there is no sun, to lie near something warm. When they move, dragons tend to move very slowly. It is only when forced that they move fast, and then, of course, they move very fast indeed.

CHAPTER
NINE

UNDER SIEGE

L eira stopped short about fifty feet from the library tower.

Something was different. The teepee—that was it. The teepee had disappeared. Either Mr. Bailey had left, which seemed very unlikely, or the teepee had escaped on its own, which seemed even more un—No, there it was. It was just that it had come unleashed and was now hovering behind a boulder, as if it were hiding.

Perhaps it sensed danger.

Three more uniformed guards from the ship were standing at strategic points around the perimeter of the building. They carried walkie-talkies on their hips and rifles over their shoulders. They looked like they were protecting the place.

But from what? Whom were they keeping out?

Unless they were keeping people *in*.

Leira's heart started thumping. She should have known. They weren't guarding the library; they were laying siege to it. She could tell by the way they kept looking into the library windows instead of surveying the landscape.

Her instincts told her to run away, but she couldn't. She had to tell Mr. B what she knew about Brett and his father.

The only tower entrance that wasn't kept locked was the front door. Unfortunately, that was also the most visible point of access. The one place the guards were certain to see her.

If the guards had been carrying keys to the tower, she simply could have pickpocketed the keys and let herself in. Or perhaps not simply (as a rule, pickpockets prefer crowded spaces with lots of places to hide; here, the conditions were the exact opposite), but you couldn't always choose your battles. Alas, the guards were interlopers, not janitors. They had no keys.

Was there another way she could use her skills?

Yes! Leira allowed herself a small smile. No doubt about it, she was a criminal mastermind.

She hid behind a bush, waiting. As soon as one of the guards walked by, she crept out behind him. It occurred to her that she'd never stolen anything from somebody carrying a rifle, or any kind of weapon at all, but she squelched the thought. There was no reason the rifle should make her job any more difficult—assuming, that is, that the guard didn't see her.

Quietly, she matched the guard's stride and then

pulled his walkie-talkie out of its holster, replacing it immediately with a small stone she'd picked up. The guard never looked over. Or down. Or any way but forward.

A second later, Leira stepped out of view and exhaled. Hopefully, she'd never have to come so close to a gun again.

Pressing down the talk button, she spoke into the walkie-talkie in a deep, low voice. "Quick! There's somebody at the back of the library. I think it's the boy. Go! Now!"

She released the button, and there was a burst of static.

The two guards who still had their walkie-talkies immediately started running to the far side of the tower. The other guard looked around in confusion, then started running as well. Not quite believing her success, Leira tossed the walkie-talkie into the grass and walked straight through the front door. She would have laughed if she hadn't been so nervous.

The first person Leira saw inside the library was Nurse Cora. Or, more precisely, the first head of hair. Nurse Cora was exceptionally short, but her hair, which was straight and silver, was exceptionally long, making her look a bit like a walking wig.

"Nurse C!" Leira whispered in her ear, or near where she thought the ear might be.

"Leira?" The nurse pulled her hair aside and looked up at Leira. "What's wrong, sweetheart?"

"That's what *I* was going to ask!" said Leira. She kept her voice low, as one did in hostage situations and, of course, libraries. "Is everyone okay?"

"Yes, I think so. Why wouldn't they be?" Cora scratched a spot that might have been the back of her neck. "Except for that poor boy from the ship. Nobody seems to be able to find him. I'm afraid he may not have made it."

"So you're not all, like, prisoners, then?" asked Leira awkwardly.

"Prisoners? What do you mean?" Nurse Cora frowned.

"Nothing. Never mind."

Behind the nurse, campers and counselors were congregated in groups, talking about the search. Certainly, nobody seemed unduly alarmed. Maybe she'd only imagined that the camp was being held hostage. Leira felt a little silly for having taken such dramatic measures in order to gain entry.

"Where's Mr. B? I have to talk to him about something."

The nurse pointed down to the bottom floor. "That way, but I wouldn't bother him unless it's very important."

"It is."

The nurse, or rather her hair, nodded.

As Leira made her way down to Mr. Bailey, the library doors opened again, and a suntanned, barrel-chested man barged in. Two men accompanied him, rifles at the ready.

"Who's in charge in here?" he demanded, smiling wide. "I want to speak to the commander in chief. Mano a mano."

"I suppose that would be me," said Mr. Bailey jovially from below. "Although I wish these campers would treat me like it. Being a commander in chief isn't what it used to be!"

Leira tried to attract his attention as he walked past her on his way to greet their visitor, but he appeared not to notice.

"Glad to meet you." The visitor clasped Mr. Bailey's hand and shook vigorously. "Brett Perry, at your service—"

"You're the father? Oh my, you must be frantic." Mr. Bailey clucked sympathetically while simultaneously extracting his hand from Brett senior's vise-like grip. "What a terrible thing to happen!"

"What? Oh, yes . . . terrible."

He doesn't sound very worried about his son, thought Leira, listening from a safe distance. Maybe Brett's father really was as heartless as Brett made him out to be.

Brett senior glanced at the shelves around them. "Crikey, that's a lot of dead trees! Guess nobody

here ever heard of an e-book?...
Kidding!"

He slapped Mr. Bailey on the shoulder. The camp director cringed.

"But seriously, this Randolph Price character, he was a smart man," Brett senior continued. "Must have been, to make so much money. I should know, right?" He chuckled modestly. "You can't tell me he spent so much time and capital building this place just to throw a bunch of old books inside."

Mr. Bailey reddened. "Some of these old books are very—" He stopped himself from finishing the sentence.

"Very what? Valuable?" Brett senior laughed. "Don't worry, they're safe from me." He picked a book off a shelf and gave it a pat. A cloud of dust billowed from it. He tossed the book over his shoulder. "You couldn't pay me to take one of these old piles of dust."

"Well, I'm grateful for that," said Mr. Bailey drily.

Brett senior smiled affably. "Now, tell me, square biz, what did Price really want with this island?"

Mr. Bailey shrugged. "To get away from it all, I suppose? Peace and quiet."

"So he builds himself a house in the path of a volcano?" Brett senior scoffed. "That sounds real peaceful." His smile disappeared, and his voice lowered an octave. From where she stood, Leira had to strain to hear. "You know what I think? I think there's another reason he came to this island, and I think you know what it is...."

"I don't understand what you mean," said Mr. Bailey, stone-faced.

"Don't be coy," Brett senior snapped. "Where is it?"

Everybody in the library seemed to stand up straight at once. Did he mean the Tree Room? Leira wondered. Had Mr. B been right to worry about the grimoires after all? Is that what Operation St. George was about?

"Where is what?" said Mr. Bailey, casually stepping between Brett senior and the banyan tree that hid the Tree Room. "I thought you were searching for your son."

"My son? I know where my son is—at the bottom of the ocean! And unless you believe in miracles, that's where he's staying."

Leira winced.

"Now, tell me where the nest is, old man!"

"Nest?" said Mr. B, keeping his voice level. "We have quite a few parrots on the island...."

"I didn't come all this way to get pooped on by some noisy little bird." Brett senior's eyes flashed angrily. "I'm talking about the biggest, baddest beast this world has ever seen, and I'm the knight in shining armor who's going to bring it to its knees!"

A dragon! thought Leira. Clay was right—he's hunting a dragon!

With everyone else's attention fixed on Brett's brutish father, Leira slipped through the crowd, avoiding her counselor Adriana's questioning glance, until she found her sister on the other side of the room. They squeezed each other's hands; their earlier fighting was forgotten in the present crisis.

"I'm sorry, I can't help you with your quest, as noble as it may be," said Mr. Bailey coolly.

"Oh, I think you can," said Brett senior.

He jerked his head; his men raised their rifles. It was a threat, to Mr. Bailey and everyone else inside the library.

Leira froze.

"Put those things down," Mr. Bailey said, sounding cross for the first time.

"Oh, we'll put things down, all right. How many people you got in here? That's a lot of bullets, but I have plenty to spare. Unless you've already changed your mind?"

Mr. Bailey didn't flinch. "If you're referring to the creature I think you're referring to, you're a bit late. There hasn't been one spotted on this island for a thousand years, and even then—"

"Then you'll just have to turn back the clock, won't you?" Brett senior interrupted. "Aren't you some kind of wizard? That's what they say."

Leira could feel the shock of everyone around her. An outsider knew there was magic on the island, or at least suspected it.

If Mr. Bailey was equally surprised, he didn't show it. "It would take a very powerful wizard to turn back time," he observed.

"Wait!" Brett senior raised a finger in the air and put a phone to his ear. Leira noticed that the phone looked identical to Flint's. Her eyes narrowed.

"What now?" He listened for a few seconds, and then a smile crossed his lips. "Okay, don't move until I get there."

He clicked off and looked at Mr. Bailey. "I might be keeping those bullets after all. But nobody is leaving this building until we get what we came for."

"And what's that?" asked Mr. Bailey.

"My son, of course." Brett senior beckoned to his guards. "You two stay here...."

As the doors closed behind Brett's father, Mira tugged on her sister's sleeve.

Silently, Mira led Leira away from the crowd and into the library bathroom.

"What are we doing?" Leira whispered. "I have to talk to Mr. Bailey."

"You want to be trapped in there with those guys pointing guns at you, or do you want to get out?" Mira whispered back. "Look—"

Mira, who had spent more time in the library than any of the other campers, pushed on a section of the tile wall.

After a moment it gave way, revealing itself to be a hidden door.

Leira stared. "Are you kidding me?"

Secrets within secrets within secrets—that was the Price Public Library.

She shook her head and peered through the doorway.

There was a dark, rocky tunnel on the other side.

"It leads to the ruins," Mira whispered. "There are matches and candles a few feet down. We'll be fine."

Leira just looked at her.

Mira shrugged. "Well, maybe not fine. But we'll be okay. Maybe."

"What about everyone else?" said Leira. "We can't just leave them."

"If those guys catch us leading anybody out, they'll shoot. We can do more good outside."

Leira looked as if she were about to accuse Mira of being selfish. "You're right," she said instead. "Let's go."

She ducked and entered the tunnel without another word.

CHAPTER
TEN

UNDERGROUND

It's not as unlikely as it might seem that Clay and Leira should enter tunnels at the very same time. In fact, a vast network of tunnels crisscrossed Price Island, some of them known to the campers, but most not. These tunnels, more properly called lava tubes, were formed by rivers of lava so powerful that they bored straight through solid rock; and they provided secret underground roadways for those who wanted to traverse the island without exposing themselves to skies—or eyes—above.

It was wonderfully convenient. It was also nature.

The lava tube in which Clay now found himself was not overly long, but it twisted and turned in a way that made for slow travel. Thankfully, the tube's ceiling and walls had been chipped away in places to make passage easier, and footholds and handholds had been carved out of the rock where required. There were even a few spots that looked like they were designed to hold lanterns or to store food or equipment. Some very determined people had put a lot of time and effort into the tunnel—under the assumption, no doubt, that they would be using it for many years to come.

He wondered what had happened to them. Where their lanterns and food and equipment were now.

As he made his way through the tunnel, though, Clay began to see signs of a different sort of activity.

A distinctly nonhuman sort of activity.

With growing apprehension, he noted claw marks at points where the tunnel had been widened well beyond what would have been necessary for a person. Repeated scratching and scraping had created bowl-shaped spaces that would have been too large for even the tallest of human beings but that were perfect for a bigger animal to curl up inside. The tunnel called to mind a giant rabbit warren—although Clay suspected that rabbit paws, even giant ones, would not be strong enough to carve through the volcanic rock.* Some bigger, sharper-clawed creatures had laid claim to this tunnel.

Much bigger, much sharper-clawed.

---

* THERE WERE, IN FACT, A FEW VERY LARGE, AND VERY UNFRIENDLY, WILD RABBITS ON THE ISLAND, BUT THEY WERE MOSTLY KEPT IN CHECK BY THE EVEN LARGER AND EVEN UNFRIENDLIER WILD PIGS.

Who survived? That was the question that plagued him. Had the humans outlasted these other creatures? Or had these other creatures outlasted the humans? And if the creatures had prevailed, as Mr. B had suggested, could one still be alive?

Could there be a dragon—it still sounded crazy to say it—living on Price Island to this very day?

Clay tried to think rationally. If there were a dragon on the island, wouldn't there have been signs? Burning trees. Animals fleeing in terror. The bloody remains of a dragon meal.

The island seemed too small to hold such a big secret.

And yet if there was one thing Clay had learned about Price Island, it was that there was always another surprise waiting around the corner.

At first, the air in the tunnel was fairly cool, except for periodic sulfurous blasts of heat that grew more and more intense as Clay pushed deeper and deeper into the mountain. There must have been another steam vent somewhere in the tunnel.

He had been walking for about ten minutes, the tunnel getting hotter and hotter all the while, when that strange, syrupy sleepiness hit him again, with even more force than before.

What was it about these caves that made him so drowsy?

Bleary-eyed, he could see a circle of light up ahead. Daylight or flashlight?

Actually, it looks more like firelight, Clay decided. Or am I just too tired to tell the difference?

He staggered toward the light, unsure whether the glow was real or a trick of his imagination. Then he stumbled, dropping his torch—

He is flying again. Over the bamboo forest.

He is high enough that the forest looks like a field of bright green grass. Yet low enough to see the bamboo bending in the wind.

There is a shadow moving across the bamboo. It looks like the shadow of an airplane, but an airplane that swings its tail and flaps its wings.

It is his shadow, he realizes.

The tail is his tail. The wings are his wings.

The wind bending the bamboo—it is his wind.

He is a dragon, and yet he is still Clay.

(In the same way, he knows he must be dreaming, and yet feels sure that he is not.)

He flaps harder. The strength in his wings is tremendous.

The bamboo bends further, bowing to his power.

The island looks different from this height, but he knows where he is. Behind him is Bamboo Bay. To his left is Mount Forge. Soon he will see Earth Ranch. . . .

Yes, there, just ahead, is the long, crescent-shaped lake. Lava Lake, it's called. And there, jutting out of the lake, is the boulder, Egg Rock, that the campers have to reach in order to pass their swim tests.

But on the shore, he sees only a few unfamiliar grass huts and a smoldering campfire. Where is everything else?

He flies low over the lake, coming up on camp. Or where camp should be.

The dome is gone. The yurts are gone. The barn: gone.

He flies faster.

The palace ruins and the library tower: gone and gone.

He glances back—even the rainbow is gone.

Something horrible has happened.

Zing! An arrow whizzes by on his right.

Zing! Zing! On his left, this time. Closer and closer.

Startled, he looks down to the bluff where Price Palace once stood, and sees a man readying his bow to shoot again. The man has paint on his face, and he is wearing some kind of skirt or loincloth. He doesn't look like anybody Clay knows from the island. Or anywhere else, for that matter. He looks like a man from a different world. A man from long ago.

That's why the camp isn't there, Clay thinks. It hasn't been built yet....

But by now Clay's voice is very faint in his head—as if his human self were disappearing over some faraway horizon. Soon it is all but obliterated by a terrible animal rage.

He comes down on the hunter like a firestorm....

CHAPTER
ELEVEN

A PRIMAL WHEEZE

Wake up, Clay. You hear me? Wake up!"

It felt like hours, but it was less than a minute later that Clay blinked awake—only to see a bow tie inches from his face. He was lying on the ground, and Brett was shaking him, just as Clay had shaken Brett on the beach the day before.

"Wake up!"

"I'm up, I'm up," Clay groaned.

"You okay?"

"No....Yes....Maybe. Just let go of me, would you?"

Brett laughed, letting go of Clay's shoulders. "Now you know what it feels like....Just don't puke on me."

"Why not? I owe you one," Clay joked groggily.

He smiled—or tried to—and sat up.

They were at one end of a vast, glittering cave, suffused with a soft orangey glow. The glow came from the long, fiery lava pit that was about twenty feet away from them.

"Why are the walls so bright?" he asked.

"Look closer—"

Clay leaned forward. His vision was a little blurry, but the sight was spectacular nonetheless. "Wow...crystals?"

Brett nodded. "Not just that. Diamonds, I think."

"How do you know?"

"I was into geology when I was little."

The diamonds were encrusted on the jagged black rock in clusters, like barnacles on a ship. They reflected a myriad of colors, but predominantly the orangey light of the lava. The color looked oddly familiar to Clay, as if he'd been in the cave before.

"Diamonds sometimes pop up around volcanoes," Brett explained. "They grow over billions of years, way down in the earth's mantle, where it's superhot and there's a lot of pressure. Then one day volcanic eruptions bring them up to the surface, and...bling! It's an overpriced engagement ring."

"Awesome."

Next to Clay was Flint's bamboo torch, no longer lit. He picked it up off the ground, then stood—and grabbed his forehead.

"Head rush, right?" said Brett. "It's the drop in blood pressure. Kind of the reverse situation of a volcano."

"Yeah, I guess..."

"Careful—"

Clay removed his hand from his eyes—just in time to avoid hitting his head against a rock formation that was hanging from the ceiling.

"That's a stalactite, in case you're wondering. As opposed to a stalagmite, which is the one that comes up from the ground. There are lots of stalactites in volcanic caves. Made from dripping lava. They're called *lavacicles*."

"Like icicles? That's funny."

Still in a daze, Clay leaned against the cave wall.

Brett smiled. "No such thing as lava-lagmites, though. Lava doesn't really make stalagmites."

Clay laughed. "You know what? You kinda remind me of my brother."

"How?"

"Just, there's a lot of stuff in your head, let me put it that way."

Brett made a face. "Too much, you mean, right?"

"What do I know? I can't keep anything in my head."

"So you and your brother..." Brett hesitated. "You're not really close then?"

Clay looked at him askance. "I didn't say that...."

Anyway, he's a lot older, and I don't even know where he is right now."

"Oh...I never had a brother. I had a stepsister. She was my best friend—well, kind of my only friend—but then..." Brett made a chopping motion with his hand.

"She was killed?!"

"No! My dad divorced her mom, that's all," said Brett. "We still text sometimes, but she's... older now."

"I know what you mean," said Clay. At their age, girls sometimes inexplicably got older in a way that boys usually didn't. It was unnerving.

"Hey, isn't that a...lava-lagmite right there?" Clay pointed at a crystal-encrusted rock formation rising out of the cave floor. "See that one that looks like a guy holding a spear?"

"I think it *is* a guy holding a spear..." said Brett.

"Like, a real guy?"

"A real spear, anyway."

They walked closer, although not much closer. It was extremely creepy.

"See how the end is sticking out?" said Brett. "It's like it was frozen in place...."

"Or burned in place," said Clay darkly.

"By lava, you mean?"

"Maybe."

"What else?"

Clay shrugged. He couldn't quite bring himself to say it: *By a dragon*.

Brett shuddered. "Maybe it's just a stalagmite after all," he said hopefully, turning away from it.

"Yeah, maybe." Or maybe not.

"Anyway, I know you probably want to hear me talk about rocks for another five hours, but can we... go?"

"Sure," said Clay, although he felt strangely reluctant to leave. "But can I at least look around a little more first?"

Without waiting for an answer, he started walking toward the lava pit.

As Clay looked from one side to the other, he couldn't escape the feeling that he'd been there before, and as soon as he got to the edge of the pit, he knew why. It was because he *had* been there before. In a dream.

He stared at the bubbles, popping and steaming when they reached the lava's surface, and he inhaled their familiar sulfurous scent. He watched the lava's constantly blackening and un-blackening crust, remembering how fantastic it had felt to dive underneath...

"Clay? You're standing a little close, aren't you?"

"What? Oh yeah." He stepped back. "Sorry, I guess I haven't totally woken up yet."

Brett looked at him with concern. "Seriously, you're acting kind of weird. I think we should get out of here."

Clay forced himself to focus. "Right. Let's go, then."

"Yeah, let's," said Brett. "The battery in my flashlight went out just before I saw you, but you've got one, right?"

"A flashlight? No, just this—" Clay held up the unlit torch. A thin wisp of smoke rose from it.

"You have a match?" asked Brett.

"Nope."

"How'd you light it before?"

"Someone else did," said Clay, in a way that didn't invite further questioning. Although, really, Clay wondered, what was the point of hiding magic from Brett anymore?

"So we're out of luck, then," said Brett grimly. "No way to get back except by feel . . . which is pretty much impossible."

"Pretty much."

"Perfect. Headline: *Twelve-year-old boy is pushed off ship and narrowly escapes drowning, only to perish under a volcano.*" Brett shook his head, as if he'd expected nothing less. "At least it makes a good story. Not that I'll ever get to tell it—"

"Oh, come on. Nobody's perishing," said Clay. "There's got to be a way to get this lit again."

"I know," said Brett. "What if we dip it in the lava? Maybe it will catch fire."

Clay shook his head. "Too risky. The whole stick might burn. What about a piece of paper?" he said, thinking of the way the leaf had caught fire in his dream. "Maybe we could light the torch with it."

"Do you see any paper?"

"Wait, I know!" Clay gestured to Brett's bow tie. "Wouldn't you be happier with that thing off anyway?"

"No way!" said Brett. "This tie is my good-luck charm. It kept me from drowning."

"Right. And it will keep you from dying under a volcano if we can use it to light the torch," said Clay. "Then it will *really* be a good-luck charm."

"Fine," Brett grumbled. He untied his bow tie and tossed it to Clay.

Clay tied it to the unlit torch, then lowered the loose end into the pit. The tie started smoking before it touched the lava. By the time it grazed the lava's surface, it was on fire.

Clay slowly raised the torch and waved it from side to side.

For the first time he noticed the enormous undulating mounds of rocks that surrounded the entire left side of the lava pit; it looked like a giant toddler had dribbled rocks through his fingers.

"Great," said Brett, turning around. "Now let's get out of here—"

"Watch out!" exclaimed Clay. "Those steam vents there will fry you if you're not careful."

He nodded in the direction of two round holes in the closest rock mound. A blast of scorching-hot air came out of them.

"See what I mean?"

Brett studied the holes, his eyes narrowing.

"Those aren't steam vents," he said quietly.

"Yeah, they are," Clay insisted. "I know you're the geology guy, but I've been on this island longer. Volcanic gas and stuff comes out of them—"

"Do steam vents suck air in before air comes out?" asked Brett, his face pale.

"No..." Clay stuck his hand out.

Brett was right: There was a slight vacuum-like pull.

"Do they move and, uh, twitch, like they're feeling itchy?"

"No..." said Clay, feeling less confident.

It was true: The holes were quivering. A bit.

"And do...big globs of green goo drip out of them?"

"No..." Clay tilted his head.

He had thought the green stuff was another, smaller rock formation, but now that Brett mentioned it...

"I see what you're saying," said Clay, his throat suddenly dry.

He noticed that his leg was jiggling and forced it to stop.

"I'm saying it's time to run for our lives," said Brett. "Screaming."

"Maybe we should try backing away slowly first," said Clay. "No screaming."

"Okay. Slowly. Right."

Brett took a step backward and—"Aaack!"—hit his head. He had backed up against the cave wall.

"I know," he said, wincing with pain. "You said no scream—"

He froze. Clay froze.

The mound with the two holes was shaking. Rocks and crystals slid off the top in a noisy avalanche.

"Volcanic eruption?" Brett whispered.

"I don't think so," Clay whispered back. "Maybe an earthquake?"

Brett shook his head. No, not that either.

As the mound's shaking lessened, a terrible sound could be heard blaring out of the two holes. A sound that must have been building for a long, long time. A sound that seemed to come from the mountain's very core. And yet, you wouldn't have described the sound as deep; it was more high-pitched.

Have you ever heard of a primal scream?* This was like that, but, well...nasal.

A primal wheeze.

The wheeze echoed throughout the cave, louder and louder, until the holes twitched for a last time, the mound heaved upward in a final spasm, and—in one big, powerful blast—sizzling-hot green goo erupted from the holes and splattered the cave.

It was as if the mountain itself had expelled its mucus.

A primal sneeze.

Or, as Brett put it, with a horrified gasp: "It's like a nose volcano."

Clay nodded, awestruck. "Snot lava."

Thankfully, they had stepped far enough away to avoid the worst of it. Still, backed up against the cave wall as they were, they had not totally escaped. Steaming globs of goo dripped from their heads, leaving behind the smell of burning hair, and oozed down their arms, leaving trails of red, blistered skin.

The burns must have hurt, but they didn't notice. Their attention was on something else.

"Are those what I think they are?" Brett mumbled. "I mean, they *are* rocks...right?"

---

* IN THE 1970S, SEEMINGLY SANE AND MATURE GROWN-UPS WOULD TRY TO CONFRONT THEIR CHILDHOOD TRAUMAS BY SCREAMING AT THE TOP OF THEIR LUNGS. THIS LOUD AND NOT NECESSARILY VERY EFFECTIVE FORM OF THERAPY WAS POPULARIZED IN A BOOK CALLED *THE PRIMAL SCREAM*.

As the last bits of rubble fell away from the mound, revealing a crusty gray under-layer, two round rocks—or what *looked* like two round rocks—had become visible a few feet behind the two steam-holes-that-weren't-steam-holes. The rocks—*if* that's what they were—appeared to be lodged in the mound's surface, as if they'd been pushed most, but not all, of the way in. Deep circular wrinkles surrounded them like ripples, and a line—or more accurately, a slit—divided each one in half.

Brett and Clay watched, riveted, as the slits started to open.

"No, definitely not rocks," said Clay.

The slits opened further. Inside, protected by heavy folds of ancient, armored skin, were two glassy, golden orbs with big, black, diamond-shaped pupils in the center.

The "rocks" were *eyes*.

There is an old saying that goes, *Just as a camel has two humps, a dragon has two hearts—one good and one bad.*

Hogwash.

I suppose it is possible that dragons have two blood-pumping organs in their bodies. (I have spent my life among dragons, yet much of their biology remains a mystery to me.) But remember this: It is people who have good hearts and bad hearts. For a dragon, there is no good or bad. There is no should or should not. There are only *is* and *is not.*

Although dragons are infinitely smarter than people, they are also simpler. Push a dragon and it will push back. Treat a dragon gently and it will treat you gently. Try to kill a dragon and it will try to kill you.

No, it *will* kill you.

This is not justice. Nor is it unjust. It just is.

CHAPTER
TWELVE

THE RUINS

Perhaps Brett senior was right, and a proximity to dragons was Randolph Price's secret reason for building such an enormous and extravagant residence on such a remote and treacherous island. But dragons or no dragons, the location proved to be a mistake. Price Palace may have taken years to complete, but when Mount Forge erupted, it was swept away in minutes.

The massive lava flows leveled not just the mansion but also all the trees and greenery and everything else that surrounded it. Now, seventy years later, there wasn't much left beyond a few columns, a broken wall, and a statue or two.

One of the few traces of the palace that remained fully intact was a square metal drain strategically hidden behind a boulder. Actually, it wasn't so much a drain as a trapdoor, as anybody who happened to see the two red-haired sisters emerging from it that afternoon would have noticed. Alas, the sisters themselves couldn't see much one way or another; the bright light was blinding after the darkness of the tunnel.

"This place always reminds me of the Parthenon," said Mira, shielding her eyes with her hand.* "Or maybe Mount Olympus."

Leira looked blank and shook her head.

"You know, ancient Greece? Greek gods...?"

Still shaking her head, Leira put her finger to her lips.

"Let me put this in terms you'll understand," said Mira. "Just think of where Wonder Woman comes from. That island—"**

---

* A temple to the goddess Athena, the Parthenon is by far the most famous example of ancient Greek architecture and a symbol of Greek civilization at its peak. (A symbol that has been robbed and pillaged shamelessly.) Like many rich and self-important people of his time, Randolph Price built his home in a style meant to recall the ancient world, and the Parthenon in particular. But to most people, I suspect, his house more closely resembled a bank or a courthouse—one of those "neoclassical" buildings that seem designed for the express purpose of making you feel small and insignificant

** The island Mira is referring to is Themyscira, also called Paradise Island, which sounds like Price Island (but possibly more expensive). According to DC Comics and some Greek pottery, Themyscira was the home of the Amazons, the all-female warrior tribe of ancient Greece. Not to be confused with the Amazon River, which derives its name from the same source. Nor with the giant, bookselling website, which, though seemingly

"Shh!" Leira whispered. "I think I hear some-body."

"Oh!" Mira put her hand to her mouth.

They listened; the ruins were silent. Then a bird suddenly squawked and flew away.

Mira tapped Leira on the shoulder. Somebody was peering out from behind a half-fallen column. The sisters peered back.

For a moment, nobody moved.

Then the person behind the column cracked a smile. "Oh, it's you guys!" he said, stepping out into the open. "What are you doing here?"

It was Jonah.

He was followed by Kwan and Pablo.

"Jeez. You scared the heck out of us!" said Mira.

"Sorry," said the Worms in chorus.

Leira explained how she and Mira had escaped from the library. "What about you? How'd you get out?"

"We didn't," said Kwan. "We were late for the meeting because we decided to check a few spots down below Bamboo Bay—in case that kid was a floater."

"When we saw those guys guarding the library, we made tracks," said Pablo.

INVINCIBLE, MAY YET SOMEDAY FALL PREY TO A VENGEFUL TRIBE OF WAR-RIOR WOMEN OUT TO RECLAIM THEIR RIGHTFUL NAME.

"Good thinking," said Leira grimly. "You didn't know how right you were about this place being a prison."

"Yo, dudes—" Jonah pointed to a large black helicopter flying overhead. It had two propellers and looked like it was built for battle. "What's that thing dangling from that chopper?"

"That's not just a chopper—that's a Chinook," said Pablo. "Military-style."

"Okay, if you say so," said Jonah. "What's that thing dangling from that *Chinook?*"

"It looks like a train car," said Kwan, squinting. "Or a shipping container."

Pablo nodded, as if this had only confirmed his suspicions. "They're probably smuggling contraband onto the island. Like child slaves. Or a nuclear weapon..."

"Not a weapon, a *dragon*," said Leira. "It's a dragon cage."

"A what?" said her sister.

"A dragon cage."

"They're smuggling a *dragon* onto the island?" said Kwan, incredulous.

"*Off* the island," said Leira.

"Like a *Komodo* dragon?" asked Jonah.

Leira shook her head. "Like a *dragon* dragon. Come on, everybody, we have to get to the dragon cave. Now!"

"The where...?" said Mira, who was beginning to worry her sister had lost her mind. "I thought you said dragon *cage*."

"I did. I'll explain on the way!"

The campers looked at one another. What in the world was Leira talking about?

Even running most of the way, it took them over twenty minutes to reach the vicinity of the cave, at which point they had to slow down to avoid detection.

Stealthily, one after another, the campers scrambled up the rocks above and to the side of the cave.

They stopped only when they found a place where they were protected by shadow but had a view of the cave entrance and the small plateau in front of it.

The shipping container was on the ground, and the helicopter had already returned with its next piece of dangling cargo: a big yellow crane, folded into itself. At the moment, the helicopter was hovering low while Brett's father's men worked to unhook the crane from its chains.

"See those holes in the side of the container?" said Leira over the sound of the helicopter. "I told you it was a cage."

"Yeah, a big freaking cage for a big freaking animal," said Kwan.

"A dragon," said Leira.

Kwan laughed. "Whatever you say."

Mira gestured to three men who were carrying bundles of short sticks into the cave. "What's that? Dynamite?"

"Yup," said Pablo, who was fairly expert in explosives.

Mira looked horrified. "They're going to blow up the cave? Why?"

Pablo shrugged. "Make it wider, maybe? For that... *big freaking animal*."

"Say they're really looking for a dragon, just for the sake of argument," said Jonah, who kept studying the cave entrance as though he were seeing inside—which his friends knew he very well might be. "What makes them think they're going to find one in there?"

Leira pointed. "Him, I'm guessing."

Below, just outside the cave, Flint was talking animatedly to one of Brett's father's men. (Brett would have recognized him as Mack, his father's bodyguard.)

"They gave him a phone," said Leira. "That's probably all it took for him to sell out the whole camp."

Jonah's eyes narrowed. "Well, that part I believe.... What a jerk."

Now free of the container, the helicopter rose higher in the air and started circling at a distance.

As the sound of the helicopter faded, they could hear Flint's furious voice echoing in the rocky canyon. "But they said they'd take me with them! We had a deal!"

"Well, the deal changed, kid!" Mack shouted back. "Now get out of the way before we blow you up along with the cave!"

Listening, Leira let out a gasp.

"What's wrong?" Mira asked.

"I just realized," said Leira. "Clay is probably still inside. And that kid Brett, too."*

---

* THE STORY OF BRETT'S DISCOVERY HAD BEEN SLIGHTLY EASIER FOR HER FRIENDS TO SWALLOW THAN THE IDEA THAT HIS FATHER WAS HUNTING A DRAGON—BUT ONLY SLIGHTLY.

"They're inside with the dragon, you mean?" said Jonah.

Kwan stared at him. "Wait—you believe her now?"

Jonah pulled at his Afro uncomfortably.

It was Leira's turn to be surprised. "Really? It's down there?"

Mira shook her head. "You're the one who keeps saying—"

"I knew there was *supposed* to be a dragon," said Leira. "I didn't know there actually was one."

Everyone looked at Jonah for confirmation.

"There's *something* down there—that's all I know."

He glanced again at the cave entrance, then closed his eyes, concentrating. The others waited nervously, knowing that his visions were not always easy to summon.

"Well, are they going to be okay?" asked Leira, unable to stand it any longer.

"Yeah...I think so," said Jonah.

"You think? That's not good enough," said Mira anxiously. "You have to be sure."

"They're caught between a dragon and a bunch of dynamite!" Jonah protested. "How sure can I be?"

Everybody looked at the mountainside, their faces somber. You didn't have to be psychic to picture all the destruction that was about to be wreaked underneath.

CHAPTER
THIRTEEN

AMBER

The captain's quarters on the *Imperial Conquest* looked much as I imagine the captain's quarters must look on any other cruise ship: that is, like a suite in an overpriced, poorly decorated hotel. (Have I told you how I feel about cruises?)

If you ask me, Captain Abad was fighting a losing battle, but she had done her best to personalize her stateroom with art and mementos from her travels. An Indonesian wave-pattern batik was hanging above her bed; a pair of Japanese temple dogs sat on either side of her desk (stone temple dogs, not living ones); and a photo of the captain as a young girl holding a sailing trophy was on the shelf. But perhaps the most notable object was the one currently in her hand: a six-foot-long wind instrument carved from a tree branch in the Australian outback.

In the past, the captain had often wondered why

she kept this oversized souvenir; she rarely blew on it, and she could never get it to sound the way it was supposed to. Now, however, she was considering the possibility that it might have a use after all: to alert her crew to her captivity. She doubted that they'd be able to rescue her, but at least they would know the score. She put her lips to the mouthpiece and blew experimentally.

All that came out was a sputter.

"Captain Abad?"

Lowering her didgeridoo to her side, the captain looked up to see a smiling young woman in a mint-green velour tracksuit entering the suite. "Welcome, Mrs. Perry."

"Oh, call me Amber, please. I'm not Mrs. Perry yet!"

"And you may call me Sofia. After all, I'm not really captaining this ship anymore, am I?" said the captain with an ironic edge to her voice.

"Oh, don't say that! I'm sure this will all be over soon," said Amber, waving away the guard who had let her into the room. He retreated a few steps but stopped beside the door. He had no intention of leaving the two women alone.

Captain Abad wasn't sure what to make of her bright and shiny guest. Rich men like Brett Perry often had young girlfriends like Amber—the captain saw it all the time on her ship—but she suspected that behind Amber's toothpaste-commercial smile there were hidden depths. Captain Abad *hoped* there were hidden depths, anyway. Her life, and the lives of her passengers and crew, just might depend on it.

"I'm sorry I don't have anything to offer you," said the captain.

"Oh, everyone eats too much on this ship," said Amber airily.

"Yes ... usually."

The only thing the captain had been given to eat that day was stale bread. She was being treated no better than a common prisoner. Why not just put her in the brig and be done with it?

"What is that ... amazing thing you're holding?" asked Amber.

"It's a didgeridoo. An aboriginal instrument. Takes great lung power. Would you like to try it?"

"Um, not right now, thank you." Amber uncapped a stick of strawberry lip balm and applied it in one quick motion.

SMOOCHIE,

it said in big letters on the side.

The captain thought the lip balm looked—and smelled—like something a four-year-old girl would choose. She hid her distaste by leaning her didgeridoo against the wall.

"So, you wanted to see me?" said Amber, recapping her lip balm.

"I just can't believe you're mixed up in all this," replied the captain. "You seem so kind, so reasonable...."

"Compared to Mr. Perry, you mean?" said Amber. "Please forgive him. He's totally out of his mind right now. You know, with his son missing and everything—"

"Of course," said the captain cautiously.

She wanted to warn Amber that her husband-to-be was a killer who had pushed his own son off the ship, but she had to gain Amber's trust first. "Well, I wanted to say thank you for asking them to untie me, that's all."

"Oh, that was just a silly mistake! I mean, imagine—what were they thinking? Is there something else I can do for you?"

"Not for me," said the captain. "But you should know that the passengers are getting restless. Some of them suspect there is more going on than a search for a missing boy. I can hear them outside my stateroom window."

"Oh?"

"You can only ply them with free booze for so long. Perhaps if you intervened with Mr. Perry, he would cut short this operation of his and concentrate on what matters now, which is finding his son—"

Amber raised her hand. "Hold on—because I think we have an itsy-bitsy, teensy-weensy little misunderstanding," she said, her smile never leaving her lips. "I so, so want to make you happy, but you see, the truth is—and I know this might be a surprise—Mr. Perry is only following my orders. Everything he does, he does because I ask him to—that sweetheart! Including, most especially, the work on Price Island."

Captain Abad stared. Amber had hidden depths after all—just not in the way that the captain had hoped.

"I know, crazy, right?" said Amber with a little giggle. "Maybe our styles are a little different, but we both command big operations. Deep down, we're the same, you and I."

"No, we're not," said the captain fiercely. "Nobody under my command has ever pushed a passenger off my ship!"

Amber's smile disappeared for the first time. "Brett junior's fall was a terrible accident," she said stiffly. "But what's that expression? To make an omelet you have to break a few eggs? Well, if we have to, we'll break a few more. If there's any trouble on this ship, any at all, the troublemakers will join Brett junior at the bottom of the ocean...and so will you. *Capeesh*, Captain?"

"Yes, I think so." The captain shivered. You don't spend your life as a sailor without hearing a lot of bloody stories, but rarely had she heard someone speak so callously of human life.

Amber's smile returned. "Fantabulous! Now, what can we do to calm down all those annoying passengers?"

At that very moment, on a lower floor of the ship, a rabbit sat behind a velvet curtain, nibbling lettuce leaves out of a top hat as if the hat were a salad bowl.

The rabbit was white and furry, a classic magician's rabbit, and the hat was black and shiny, a classic magician's hat. Sadly, the man pacing back and forth beside them, munching on a small bar of chocolate, didn't look like much of a magician, classic or otherwise. His suit was dirty and rumpled. His face pale and unshaved. His eyes tired and desperate. Judging by his appearance, nobody would ever call him the Amazing So-and-So or the Marvelous Whosie-Whatsit or Somebody-or-Other the Magnificent. In short, he was the last person you would expect to see as the headliner on a cruise-ship marquee.

Nevertheless, this magician—for magician indeed he was—had evidently impressed somebody enough to earn the all-important job of entertaining passengers on the *Imperial Conquest*, and I ask you to consider the possibility that he might have been a slightly better magician than he looked. Believe me, he had his share of critics—chief among them himself—without your contributing to the chorus. So please be kind.*

Even on a good day, the magician suffered from performance anxiety, but today his anxiety about the performance ahead was exacerbated by his anxiety about something else. (In truth, his performance anxiety was often exacerbated by anxieties of other sorts, but does that mean we should be any less sympathetic? On the contrary.) Like everyone else aboard the ship, the magician was alarmed that they were stalled in the middle of the ocean. Unlike everyone else, the magician knew a thing or two about the small volcanic island on which the ship's owner was purportedly searching for his missing son. He knew about Mount Forge and Price Palace and Earth Ranch. He even knew about the grimoires and the secret library-within-the-library. Unfortunately, what he knew did not reassure him; it made him more worried.

The magician stopped pacing and addressed the

---

* Why am I so defensive about this particular character, you ask? Funny, I wasn't aware that I was. I strive for fairness and objectivity, no matter whom I'm writing about.

rabbit. "Stop giving me the silent treatment! I'm just as upset as you are. I didn't sleep a wink last night. And you know me, when my insomnia kicks in..."

The rabbit continued to eat, ignoring him.

"How could I have known ahead of time that the ship was headed for Price Island?" the magician protested, as if the rabbit had accused him of ignoring this crucial piece of information. "We got on board to track the Midnight Sun's movements, not predict them!"

The magician reopened the chocolate wrapper in his hand and examined it. Not even a smear of chocolate left. He crumpled it in frustration.

"Yes, I know they're building a mysterious giant arena—I was the one who told you that. And our information is that it's in the desert, not on an island; that's my point.... What? Sure, I agree that deserts are dry and water is wet.... Correct: There aren't many deserts in the middle of water. So...? Then why did I think this ship was headed for a desert? I don't know, smarty-pants. Maybe I thought it would dock, and then they would drive into the desert. How 'bout that...? Aargh. Why I am even answering these questions?!"

The rabbit tossed aside a bad lettuce leaf with its teeth, then tried another one.

"Plus, I always assumed Price Island was so well protected that the Midnight Sun didn't even know about it! I know, I know, they know everything."

The magician sighed. "But what am I supposed to do now? I can't even warn the camp about who they're dealing with. Earth Ranch communications are so secure that you can't communicate with them! What do they expect? Carrier pigeons? Owls? I'm sorry, but all I've got is you. And last time I checked, you don't fly. Or swim."

He stared at the rabbit as if daring the rabbit to contradict him.

The rabbit stared back.

"Don't look at me like that! I know I'm the reason Clay is there, but Clay can take care of himself," said the obviously guilt-ridden magician. "Did you know when he was ten and I was twenty-two he was already as tall as I was? How 'bout that? It's almost like *he* was the big brother! Besides, he probably won't run into them anyway. It's not the campers that they're after."

The rabbit raised its eyebrows—or would have if it had *had* any eyebrows.

"No, I don't know what the Midnight Sun wants—that's the problem! The books, probably—"

Before the magician could speculate further, his soliloquy was interrupted by a woman's voice:

"I thought I heard somebody back here..."

Amber appeared backstage with a questioning smile.

Startled, the magician pretended to sneeze and

shielded his face with a handkerchief. Here she was: his old nemesis. He hadn't seen her since middle school. Not since before she had joined the Midnight Sun.

How much had she heard? Did she recognize him?

"Are you the magician?" she asked.

"Who—who else would I be?" he stammered as he fumblingly put on a pair of sunglasses.

"I don't know," said Amber, "but you don't look like somebody going onstage in half an hour. I don't mean to be rude, but do you maybe have a change of clothes?"

"Why? I just need to get out of the bright light, that's all—" The magician stepped into a shadow, hoping to further obscure his face. "See, isn't this better?"

"A little..." Amber gave him one of her best smiles. "I know—why don't I send someone to press your suit for you?"

"Uh, okay...thanks?" said the magician, relieved. It certainly didn't seem as though she recognized him.

"Don't mention it. My fiancé owns this ship, and a girl has to make herself useful, right?" Amber stepped closer to him. "Do I know you?"

"No!" said the magician, fighting the urge to back away. "I mean, I don't think so...."

Amber peered at him in the half-light. "What's with the sunglasses? I hope you don't have a black eye."

"Just, you know...bad night."

"Well, perk up," said Amber, turning away. "I

need you looking your best. There's a new schedule. You'll be doing your show five times tonight."

"Five times?!" the magician exclaimed, unable to hide his distress.

Amber nodded. "And it better be the performance of a lifetime! It's your job to distract the passengers."

"From what?"

"From the sad reason that we're all sitting out here in the ocean, of course," said Amber gravely. "My fiancé's son . . . ?"

"Oh, right. Sorry about that."

The magician studied her from behind his sunglasses. He had assumed that the son didn't exist. Or at least that his fall had been faked. But her face made him wonder if there was some truth to the story.

"So can I count on you?" she asked.

"Sure, okay, but I have one request," said the magician before he could think better of it.

"Yes?"

"Those chocolates they put on the pillows at night—I'll need a bowlful of them. And a few carrots for my rabbit."

"Consider it done," said Amber, about to head offstage. She turned back, frowning. "Are you sure we don't know each other?"

"Oh, I doubt we run in the same circles!" The magician fiddled with a box of props, hiding his face. "Actually, I don't run in any circles," he joked nervously. "I just...run in circles....Get it? Like a dog runs in circles?"

Before Amber could respond, an aide walked up to her.

"Ma'am? Mr. Perry sent a message. He said they're inside the mountain, and they found proof—it's in there."

Amber's smile returned. "That's amazing news! I have to call France. Antoinette will want to hear right away..."

After Amber walked off, the magician looked down at the rabbit, which was burrowed inside the hat.

"How 'bout that? Ten years later and just as horrible as ever. How does she stay so...perfectly the same?" The magician shuddered; the encounter with Amber had rattled him. "Do you remember that school talent show when I made her disappear?" He sighed. "Best trick ever. Too bad it didn't last...."

The rabbit peeked its head out of the hat and glanced anxiously around the stage.

"Don't worry, she's gone," said the magician. "The real question is, what's inside that mountain and why is she so excited about it? For some reason, I don't think it's library books...."

The magician pulled the crumpled chocolate wrapper out of his pocket and looked at it as if it might hold the answer to his question.

DRAGONSLEEP

According to popular myth, a *Musca domestica*—also known as a housefly—lives for only one day.

In reality, assuming no hungry frog catches up with it, a fly may live two weeks or longer. Still, two weeks is a short life span compared to those of many other animals. Tree frogs, for example, tend to live for over twelve years—plenty of time to catch the housefly's descendants, and the descendants' descendants' descendants.

Now, dogs live slightly longer on average than frogs. No doubt you have heard that one dog year is equivalent to seven human years? I don't know that this is true in the strictest sense, but let's say it's true in a general way, and that a twelve-year-old dog is like an eighty-four-year-old person. Going back to houseflies for a moment, an equivalently elderly fly would be twelve *days* old. That is, twelve days from our human perspective. A lifetime from the fly's perspective.

In an equation, the relationship might look like this:

12-DAY-OLD 🪰 = 12-YEAR-OLD 🐕 = 84-YEAR-OLD 🧍

OR

1 🪰 DAY = 1 🐕 YEAR = 7 🧍 YEARS

OR

1 🪰 DAY = 365 🐕 DAYS = 2,555 🧍 DAYS

To put it another way, a human lives seven times as long as a dog and 2,555 times as long as a fly.

Of course, it would be presumptuous of me to pretend that I could ever truly understand a dragon's perspective on humans. (Dangerously presumptuous if a dragon ever got wind of it.) I think it is safe to say, however, that to a dragon, a human is more like a fly than like a dog. Certainly, we are more like flies in terms of our life spans.

That is, just as a person lives 2,555 times as long as a fly, a dragon lives 2,555 times as long as a person.

More or less.

If there is such a thing as dragon years to compare

to human years or dog years or fly years, the equation would go something like this:

12-DAY-OLD 🪰 = 12-YEAR-OLD 🐕 = 84-YEAR-OLD 🧍
= 214,620-YEAR-OLD 🐉

OR

1 🪰 DAY = 1 🐕 YEAR = 7 🧍 YEARS = 17,885 🐉 YEARS

OR

1 🪰 DAY = 365 🐕 DAYS = 2,555 🧍 DAYS = 6,528,025 🐉 DAYS

How do I know? I don't. It's just guesswork based on my readings on the subject.* Nobody really knows how long dragons live, or even if they age at all.

I am reasonably certain, however, that dragons sleep; and the question I am coming to via this very circuitous route is the following:

If a dragon day is 2,555 times as long as a human day, then for how long does a dragon sleep?

Assuming a human sleeps, on average, eight hours each night, and that a dragon sleeps proportionately

---

* SIDENOTE: I HOPE YOU LIKE THE SELECTIONS FROM *SECRETS OF THE OCCULTA DRACO*. THE BOOK IS ONE OF A KIND, BUT I HAVE TO CONFESS THAT READING THE WHOLE THING IS A BIT OF A CHORE. BELIEVE ME, I HAVE DONE YOU A FAVOR BY EXCERPTING SHORT PASSAGES.

as long, then a dragon would sleep for an average of 20,440 hours, or 851.6 days, or 2.3 years.

Unfortunately for my math (which has never been very good), I have reason to believe dragons sleep much, much longer than that. In effect, they hibernate.

How long? I'm glad you asked. From a physiological standpoint, dragons' closest cousins appear to be reptiles. (Although, of course, dragons predate modern reptiles by thousands of years.) Most snakes and lizards hibernate—or, technically, *brumate**—for almost half a year. That is, half a human year. That is, half the time it takes for the earth to circle the sun. Assuming a dragon hibernates proportionately as long, it would sleep for 1,277.5 years at a stretch.

And that, I think you'll agree, is a long time by any measure.

Which takes us back to our story.

When we left them, Clay and Brett were being regarded through a pair of big golden eyes. I don't think you will be surprised to hear that these eyes did not belong to a fly or a dog or even a person.

They were dragon eyes. And they had just opened after a long dragon sleep.

---

* BRUMATION: BEING COLD-BLOODED (MUCH LIKE CERTAIN PEOPLE I WON'T MENTION), REPTILES LACK THE ABILITY TO WARM THEMSELVES. DURING WINTER MONTHS THEY ENTER A PERIOD OF DORMANCY SIMILAR TO THE HIBERNATION PRACTICED BY MAMMALS, NOTABLY BEARS, BUT MUCH LESS, WELL, FURRY.

How long? I can't say that it was 1,277.5 years exactly, but that number should give you an idea.

I don't know about you, but the longer I sleep, the crankier—and hungrier—I am when I awaken.

Our friends probably should have run when they had the chance.

Now their backs were against the wall.

Literally. The cave wall.

They looked at the dragon. The dragon looked at them.

Its eyes were the size of headlights. Its head was the size of a car.

A small car, perhaps. But for a head, big enough.

The dragon's many fangs stuck out of its mouth, zigzag-style, forming a zipper of teeth that made the creature look like a mutant crocodile.

A very big mutant crocodile.

The zipper hadn't opened.

Yet.

And the rest of the dragon? Still hidden under mounds of rocks.

For the moment.

We are going to die.

Clay and Brett had the same thought. There was no need to say it aloud. The dragon was going to eat them, and that was that.

They might as well have been staring at a ticking bomb.

Tick.

Tick.

Do nothing.

That was the main piece of advice Clay had garnered from *Secrets of the Occulta Draco*. Already, he could tell that the author was right: Doing nothing in the presence of a dragon was much harder than it sounded. It was like mindfulness. Only with his life hanging in the balance.

Or, rather, his death.

Tick.

Tick.

In his thoughts, Clay kept returning to his dreams. They weren't really *his* dreams, he felt sure; they were the dragon's dreams. He, Clay, had only viewed them as a guest. He remembered the dragon's fury at the hunter who had shot the arrows at the dragon, the fire that raged in the dragon's belly. Had the dragon really killed the hunter? What about the dead body in the cave—the one with the spear? Was that the last time the dragon had seen a human being?

Yes or no, it didn't bode well.

Tick.

Tick.

Clay found himself staring deeper and deeper into the dragon's eyes. He felt as though he were falling into them. He fought to stay aware of his surroundings—he suspected that the dragon was hypnotizing him—but he kept feeling drowsier...

...and drowsier...

Tick.

Tick.

...and draggier...

...and draggier...

Tick.

Tick.

...and dragon-ier...

...and dragon-ier...

Tick.

Tick.

Until he could have sworn he wasn't a boy anymore, but rather a dragon looking at a boy and about to—

Bzzzz. Bzzzzz. Bzzzzzzzzz.

A buzzing sound brought him back to the present.

"What's that?" Brett whispered.

"It sounds like a fly," said Clay.

It *was* a fly. Buzzing around one of the dragon's eyes. The dragon blinked and shook its enormous head, spilling more rocks to the ground, but the fly kept coming back, attracted to the shiny golden eye as if it were an eighty-watt lightbulb.

Although quite big by fly standards, the fly was microscopic by dragon standards. Even so, Clay could tell the dragon was irritated.

Very irritated.

Why didn't the dragon just swat the fly away? he wondered. Maybe it was too small for the dragon's big claws to catch?

And then the fly stopped flying—

—and landed on the dragon's nose.

The dragon shook its head again. More rocks and pebbles flew off.

But not the fly.

The dragon's big nostrils—now very obviously nostrils and not steam vents—twitched.

"Uh-oh. I think he's going to sneeze again," Clay whispered.

"So do something," said Brett.

"Like what?"

"I don't know—make the fly go away?"

Clay took a breath, reached out, and—

CLAP!

—smashed the fly between his palms.

Right in front of the dragon's eye.

Brett stared at him in shock. "Do you have a death wish?"

"Sorry. You said—"

"I didn't mean like *that*."

The dragon didn't blink. But its eyes narrowed a bit.*

---

* I KNOW, THE HERO OF A BOOK ISN'T SUPPOSED TO KILL AN ANIMAL, EVEN A FLY. IT'S HEARTLESS AND CRUEL AND A BAD EXAMPLE TO SET FOR YOUNG READERS. I'M SORRY. I HAD TO INCLUDE THIS TERRIBLE CRIME BECAUSE, AS YOU'LL SEE, IT PROVED VERY CONSEQUENTIAL. IT MAY EVEN HAVE SAVED CLAY'S LIFE. AND GUESS WHAT—ALL THOSE OTHER HEROES? THEIR AUTHORS MAY NOT HAVE SAID SO, BUT I BET MOST OF THEM KILLED A FEW FLIES IN THEIR TIME. OR AT LEAST STEPPED ON A FEW ANTS. I SPEAK FROM EXPERIENCE. WHEN I WAS YOUNG, I TRIED TO SPARE THE LIFE OF EVERY LIVING CREATURE I CAME ACROSS, NO MATTER HOW SMALL. BUT SOMETIMES, THROUGH NO FAULT OF YOUR OWN, YOU SIT DOWN IN THE WRONG PLACE AND—*squish!*— BYE-BYE, BUG; HELLO, GROSS STAIN ON THE SEAT OF YOUR PANTS.

CHAPTER
FIFTEEN

BOOM!

Clay just stood there in the lava cave, unable to breathe, imagining the many and various ways the dragon might kill him.

For example, the dragon might slash him open with a swipe of a claw.

Or throw him against the jagged rocks.

Or toss him into the pool of lava.

Or step on him like an ant.

The dragon might breathe fire on him, toasting Clay like a marshmallow until he was a perfect golden brown, and then nibble him slowly, bit by bit.

Or did the dragon prefer its humans more well-done?

Maybe the dragon would keep breathing on Clay until he was fully roasted, his skin charred to a crisp, and then swallow him whole?

Or maybe the dragon would just scare him to death. He was already halfway there.

And then Clay's mind cleared.

Or not cleared, exactly—more like the opposite.

Fogged. His mind fogged.

Vogged?

All thoughts of his death were gone, replaced by another thought.

Well, not a thought exactly, more like a feeling.

Not his own feeling, but a feeling he was experiencing nonetheless. In the way one experiences a temperature or a smell. Something that's around you and that affects you but that doesn't come *from* you.

It was an odd and amorphous feeling, but also a comforting feeling.

If he had to put it into words, the words would have been these:

Thank you.

The dragon was thanking him for getting rid of the fly.

Or rather, since it clearly wasn't a question of politeness, or of the dragon actually thanking anyone, maybe a better way to explain it is that the dragon was thankful, and he, Clay, was feeling the dragon's gratitude.

Then again, I doubt dragons ever feel anything as human as gratitude, so the whole thing is a bit of a mystery.

"What's going on?" Brett asked, unable to contain himself any longer. He'd been watching the strange silent exchange between Clay and the dragon, and naturally he was feeling very antsy about the outcome.

"I don't know," said Clay hesitantly. "I think maybe I . . . made a friend?"

Brett looked at him quizzically. "With *me*? Seems like a funny time to mention it, but . . . thanks?"

"With the dragon."

"Oh, right." Brett's smile faded. "I mean, obviously—"

"Oh, c'mon—" said Clay, his eyes never leaving the dragon's.

"No, no, I get it," said Brett. "So maybe he doesn't say much, but if you like the strong, silent type, and you can live with all the nose lava . . ."

Clay shook his head. "Dude, you saved my life, waking me up back there. I think that makes us friends."

"It does?" Brett brightened—whether out of happiness at being called *dude* or being considered someone's friend, or both. "Of course, you coming down here in the first place counts as saving *my* life, so—"

"We're even? Sounds like friends to me," said Clay.

"But we're really not, because you saved my life on the beach, too." Brett's smile vanished again. "Does that mean I'm unfriended?"

Clay put his finger to his lip. "Shh. The dragon's telling me something."

"With his eyes?"

"Yeah. Or his mind, I guess."

"Well, I hope his mind is saying that he decided not to eat us," said Brett, who knew he should stop talking but couldn't. (I sympathize.) "Tell him I recommend a nice eggs Benedict. It's my go-to for brunch."

"Oh! Sorry!" said Clay to the dragon, turning red.

"What did he say?"

"*She*, er, I think," said Clay, concentrating. "Or, no, actually, it says dragons aren't really male or female. *We have no use for such things*, it says."

"It talks in the royal we?"

"Um...yeah," said Clay, not entirely certain what that was.* "And I think it's saying we're supposed to call it *they*, not *it*....Sorry! I mean, we're supposed to call *them* they. It's more polite.... Also, they say I made a mistake. We're not friends. I mean, the dragon and me aren't friends, because friends are equals, and dragons are infinitely superior to humans." Clay paused, as if listening, then

---

* THE *ROYAL WE*, MORE PROPERLY KNOWN AS THE *MAJESTIC PLURAL*, IS THE USE OF A PLURAL PRONOUN BY A MONARCH—OR A PERSON WHO MERELY REGARDS HIM- OR HERSELF AS A MONARCH—TO REFER TO HIM- OR HERSELF ALONE. EXAMPLE: THE PHRASE "WE ARE NOT AMUSED," ATTRIBUTED TO QUEEN VICTORIA, WHO REPUTEDLY FOUND A DINNER GUEST'S SCANDALOUS STORY DISTASTEFUL. (I SWEAR IT WASN'T ME.)

continued. "But don't worry. It...they won't eat us. Humans don't taste very good. We have no flavor. Dragons prefer game animals. Deer...antelope..."

Brett stared, incredulous. "The dragon told you all that?"

"Kind of. It's hard to explain. I just know it. Almost like I thought it myself."

"Okay. I understand. Sort of..." said Brett, although clearly he didn't. "So does...they have a name?"

Clay nodded. "Ariella."

"Ariella? That's pretty girly, isn't it, considering...? Hey, maybe it's the dragon's drag name!" Brett laughed at his own joke. "Get it, drag-dragon?"*

"Well, I think Ariella is an *awesome* name for a dragon!" said Clay pointedly. (If *his* mind talked, it would have been saying, *Don't upset the dragon, you idiot.*) "And by the way, aren't you the one who's always complaining about bullies?"

"I wasn't being a bully! That was just a dumb joke."

Clay shrugged. "Just sayin'."

---

* Generally speaking, to dress in drag is to wear clothing opposite from what is expected for one's gender. Thus a drag queen is a man dressed like a woman, and a drag king is a woman dressed like a man. A drag name, meanwhile, is a name chosen to go along with a drag persona—the more outrageous, the better. One popular way to choose your drag name is to pair your favorite ice cream flavor with the name of your favorite pet. Mine: Chocolate Quiche, of course.

"Besides, how can you bully a dragon? That's ridiculous," said Brett. "Anyway, it's...they're the one saying we have no flavor! I take offense to that."

"Hi, Ariella," Clay said softly. "Still itchy?"

Bravely, he reached out and scratched the dragon on the nose. The dragon's scaly skin was so tough it was like scratching on the cave walls. And yet Clay felt sure that the dragon appreciated what he was doing.

Until suddenly the dragon batted Clay away with its nose and reared its head back.

Clay and Brett ducked, ready for the dragon to sneeze again.

Instead, the dragon rose on its forelegs and shook itself like a giant dog shaking off water. As Brett and Clay watched in wonder, centuries of accumulated rocks and crystals cascaded off the dragon's back.

Gone were the mounds of rocks that had taken up so much of the cave. In place of the mounds stood the dragon in all its glory. So gray and craggy was the great beast that it looked like it had been carved out of the very cave it had been sleeping in.

The dragon shook itself again, this time spreading its wings a bit and giving its tail a powerful swish.

More rocks fell to the cave floor, but with the rocks came something else. It looked like pieces of crust. Big, gray, rocky pieces of crust. Falling off the dragon's legs and tail.

Soon, even bigger pieces were falling from the

dragon's stomach and back, like sheets of old, rusty armor.

"What's it doing now?" whispered Brett.

"I don't know...shedding its skin?"

"Like a snake?"

"I guess..."

Without warning, the dragon opened its mouth. And for a moment Clay and Brett were looking at a long, forked ruby-red tongue and row upon row upon row—three rows!!!—of jagged yellow teeth.

They held their breath, fearing the worst: The dragon had decided to eat them after all!

The dragon opened wider and wider and then—so fast they felt a wind blow—clamped its jaws shut.

As Clay and Brett exhaled with relief, the dragon's face peeled off in a single, horrible piece that perfectly preserved the giant, terrifying shape of the dragon's eye sockets, nostrils, and jaws. The old gray skin hung briefly from the dragon's neck before dropping to the ground like a discarded Halloween mask.

"Whoa..." murmured Clay.

A new dragon stood before them, with scales as pale and shiny as a pearl, so smooth and slinky that you could hardly see where one scale began and another ended.

"I know, it's—I mean, they're—" Brett addressed the dragon, stammering. "I mean *you're* beautif—"

BOOM!

Clay and Brett jumped as the sound of an explosion somewhere above echoed in the cave.

The dragon didn't move, but its scales bristled as if a strong wind were passing through them.

"What was that?!" said Clay.

"Sounds like my dad," said Brett grimly. "He's always exploding stuff. Except usually he's looking for oil. Not dragons."

BOOM!!

There was another explosion, louder and closer than the first.

The dragon kept standing still. Its scales bristled again, this time briefly flushing red—a sign, Clay was sure, of anger or agitation.

"Leave," he urged the dragon. "Go! Please! Now!"

"Yeah, Ariella, shoo!" said Brett.

Clay gave him a look. "I can't believe you just told a dragon to shoo."

"Well, why isn't it moving? Ariella, bad people come! Scary! Away! Go!" said Brett, louder this time.

Clay put his fingers to his lips and listened to some inaudible signal coming from the dragon.

Suddenly, his eyes glazed over, and his voice became low and gravelly. *"There is no need to shout, puny human creature."*

Brett looked at him. "Clay? This isn't really the time for jokes."

"What have we to fear from humans?" Clay continued in the same strange voice. *"Humans presumed to hunt us before and paid the price. Your kind is no more a threat to us than a fly."**

"Sorry, it's—it's just that—" Brett stammered.

"You are scared, human?"

Brett nodded.

"Then you may stand behind us."

Clay opened his eyes. "We should stand behind Ariella."

"I know, you just said—or they did."

"You can hear Ariella, too?" asked Clay, confused. Evidently, he did not remember having Ariella speak through him.

"No...never mind," said Brett. "Let's just do what the dragon says—"

They stepped behind the dragon's legs as another explosion rocked the cave, this one closer still.

---

* Told you so! We are to dragons as flies are to us.

BOOM!!!

Closer than close.

Smoke billowed in the cave, and rocks fell around them. A bright, fiery light briefly blinded their eyes.

They could hear voices cheering. "Woo-hoo!" "Look at those crystals!" "What is this place?!"

As the smoke cleared, Clay and Brett peered out from between the dragon's legs.

Brett's father's crew had entered the cave. Holding long spearguns in their hands, and fully outfitted in fireproof suits and helmets, they looked as though they were ready to wage battle on the moon.

They shouted when they saw the dragon.

"There it is!" "What a monster!" "Look at those claws!" "And that tail!" "Stay back!"

In answer, the dragon—its skin now glowing red-orange like the lava—reared its head back and—

—roared. An intense burst of blue fire scorched

the ceiling of the cave and carried all the way to the entrance to the tunnel.

It was a warning blast only. But, oh, what a warning.

"Oh, man, that was sick," murmured Clay, awe-struck. "Did you see how blue the fire was?"

"They say blue flames are the hottest," said Brett.*

The terrified dragon hunters all took a step backward. They seemed to be unsure whether to run or fight.

"They're all going to die, aren't they?" Brett stared at them. "I wonder if my dad's with them. I mean, sure, I hate him, but..." He faltered, stricken.

Clay looked from Brett to his dad's crew, hesitating. Then he put his hand on the dragon's leg. "Ariella, please give them another chance," he whispered, unsure whether the dragon could hear him, let alone understand him. "Just scare them again—I'm sure they'll run."

The dragon narrowed its eyes to slits, looking from Brett to his father's crew, very much as Clay just had. The boys waited nervously. Judging by the low growl coming from the dragon, it wanted nothing more than to firebomb every last person in the cave.

---

* ACTUALLY, WITH ALL DUE RESPECT TO BRETT'S ENCYCLOPEDIC SCIENTIFIC KNOWLEDGE, IT WAS MORE LIKELY THE INGREDIENTS IN THE DRAGON'S BREATH, NOT THE HIGH TEMPERATURE, THAT TURNED THE FLAMES BLUE. SULFUR, AMONG OTHER CHEMICALS, HAS THAT EFFECT.

Finally, the dragon let out another big fiery roar, even bigger and fierier than the last.

But still a warning only.

The hunters did not run.

"Now!" somebody yelled. "Shoot—now!"

Suddenly, hundreds of long shining darts sailed through the air toward the dragon, like a school of needlefish attacking a sea monster.

Most rebounded off the rocks, echoing throughout the cave.

More than a few hit the dragon, however.

Enraged, the dragon stood on its hind legs and, aiming lower now, let loose a tremendous blast of fire that singed the tops of the hunters' helmets. It was not yet a direct attack, but it was something more than a warning; it was a roar to remember.

There were screams and shouting. The arm of a man's suit caught on fire, but his closest neighbor quickly doused it with a fire extinguisher.

The dragon stared, its big golden eyes blinking. Clay could tell that Ariella was even more taken aback than he was. In the dragon's experience, humans were not a fire-resistant species.

"Again!"

The hunters took advantage of the dragon's surprise, releasing a second, longer volley of darts. More of them hit their target this time, tearing the dragon's wings and hobbling its legs.

Once again, the dragon breathed fire upon its assailants, but the fire came out as a cough—more a protest of pain than a lethal weapon.

"Again!"

Clay could feel each dart as it pierced the dragon's tender new skin, and he could feel the drugs working their dark magic in the dragon's veins. He was filled with rage and despair—whether his own or the dragon's, he couldn't tell—until he found himself slipping under. . . .

Fear not—we shall see you again. The thought came to him unbidden and very faint, as if it had floated a great distance.

Brett brought him back with a sharp pinch on the arm. He pulled Clay into the shadows.

The dragon had fallen to the ground, and its long tongue was hanging out of the side of its mouth in a way that to Clay seemed like an insult to the majestic beast.

The hunters rushed over to it with heavy loops of chain in their hands, as well as the big muzzle Brett had seen on the ship.

"Quick! Before it wakes it up!" "I'm not getting near that thing!" "Just do it before I shoot you in the eye!"

As Clay and Brett watched, three very nervous men clamped the muzzle onto the sleeping dragon's jaws while others wound chains around its legs and wings.

"We have to stop them," said Clay, horrified.

"How, exactly?"

"If I can just get that muzzle off, then Ariella can—"

"First of all, you'll never get the muzzle off," said Brett. "Second, the dragon is totally unconscious—"

"I know, and it's my fault," said Clay, miserable. "I said those guys would run away."

"Uh-huh, and if you hadn't, most of them would be dead now. And they probably would have caught Ariella in the end anyway."

Now the dragon was being wrapped in an enormous tarp that connected by way of a big hook to a heavy iron chain.

The chain went taut, and the tarp started sliding across the rocky floor. Somewhere outside the mountain, a crank was turning, pulling the dragon slowly out of the cave.

Whooping, the victorious hunters held on, catching a ride.

Brett and Clay watched, aghast, no longer bothering to hide.

At the sight of them, one of the men said something into his walkie-talkie, and the dragon abruptly stopped moving. The man tore off his helmet and took a step toward our heroes. He resembled Brett only a little bit around the eyes, yet Clay knew immediately it was Brett's father.

He stared at his son in astonishment. "Brett?!"

"Yep. And still alive. Disappointed?"

"Very funny." Brett senior turned to his crew. "This here is my son, everyone! We found him after all. What are the chances? Today is my lucky day!" He turned back to Brett and opened his arms. "Come here and hug your father. I was so worried, I can't tell you."

Brett looked at him suspiciously. "I don't think so."

"What do you mean?" said his father, still smiling. "Not still sore at me, are you?"

"You could say that."

"Okay, if that's how you want to play it," said Brett senior, dropping his arms. "What the heck are you doing here, anyway?"

"Stopping you from taking that dragon," said Brett boldly. "What do you think?"

Brett's father's face turned cold. "What are you going to do, threaten to call PETA again? A lot of good that did."

Brett's lip trembled a little, but there were no tears. "You tried to kill me. A lot of good that did."

"Oh, get over it," Brett senior scoffed. "I know how good a swimmer you are. If I wanted to kill you, I would have done it another way...."

"Nobody's that good," said Brett. "I was just lucky."

His father opened his mouth to argue, but then, looking at his companions, he switched gears. Apparently, he didn't want to fight with his son in front of them. "Let's forget about all that. This is a chance to start over. Promise me you'll quit this save-the-whales nonsense. Then we'll go home and—"

"And watch you put a dragon's head on your trophy wall? No, thanks."

Brett senior laughed derisively. "Is that what you think this is about?"

"Isn't it? Or is the dragon being sold as belts and wallets? Oh, and let's not forget those dragon-skin purses and shoes. They'll be to die for!"

"If you bothered to ask instead of making your wild accusations, you'd know that Amber's friends are building a dragon sanctuary in the Kalahari Desert."

"A sanctuary?" echoed Brett, dubious. "Didn't you just tell me to stop saving the whales?"

"Only so you don't look like an idiot. Amber is a dedicated environmentalist. The whole idea is to prevent the species from going extinct."

"So *that's* why you shot a thousand darts into the dragon?"

"Come on, would *you* want to travel with a dragon that wasn't muzzled and chained?"

Brett shrugged. His father had a point.

"I still can't believe you're doing all this to save an animal. I'm sorry, but it doesn't really sound like you."

"Oh, don't worry, I haven't gone completely

soft." His father laughed. "There's money involved, too—plenty of it."

"Well, that's a relief," said Brett.

His father reddened. "What's wrong with win-win? Look, I'm sorry if I said some harsh things. I want to make it up to you, the...accident and everything." He gestured to the dragon behind him. "After we get this guy where he's going, we can go on another trip. Just you and me."

"Really?"

"Really. Wherever you want."

Brett wavered. Was it possible his father meant it?*

"Hey, boss. Look—" One of the other men pointed to the dragon. It was moving under the tarp.

"Well, shoot it again, moron!"

As another volley of darts hit the dragon, one of its long claws poked through the tarp and shredded a few inches of the heavy canvas. Then the dragon's body jerked a last time, and its movements subsided.

Clay shuddered in sympathy. Brett looked from him to the dragon to his father.

"It's now or never," Brett senior said to his son. "You don't come with me, chances are you're not getting out of here at all."

---

* WISHFUL THINKING, YOU SAY? PERHAPS. BUT PEOPLE HAVE BEEN KNOWN TO FORGIVE A LOT OF THINGS, HOPING THAT THEIR PARENTS WOULD EVENTUALLY COME AROUND AND SHARE THE LOVE THAT THEY'D BEEN WITHHOLDING.

Brett hesitated, torn between conflicting emotions and loyalties. "Will you take Clay up, too?"

Brett senior glanced at Clay. "Sorry. He's seen too much already. Can't afford the risk."

"Then never!"

Now Brett had proof his father was every bit as heartless as he had suspected.

Clay looked at him in surprise. "That's crazy. At least one of us should—"

Brett shook his head. "We're friends. Friends stick together, right? Not that I would know..."

"Very principled," sneered Brett senior. "And very stupid."

"Maybe so," said Brett. "But before you go, there's something I've been wanting to tell you...."

"Yeah? What's that?"

"Your hair plugs look terrible. You're not fooling anybody."

Brett's father clenched his jaw. "They just haven't grown in yet. Soon my hair's going to be thicker than ever. You'll see. Or maybe you won't." He raised his walkie-talkie to his mouth. "Take us up!"

He continued to bark orders to his crew as he was pulled into the tunnel along with the dragon.

The last words Clay and Brett could hear were, "Yes, I said light it, darn it!"

Thirty seconds later, there was another explosion and—

BOOM!!!!

—the entrance to the tunnel collapsed behind him.

Shocked, Clay and Brett watched rocks tumble around them; the way they'd come into the cave was no longer the way out.

CHAPTER
SIXTEEN

UP

They stared, unmoving, at what had once been the tunnel entrance. There was nothing left but rubble. And clouds of dust.

Brett kicked a boulder with his foot. It wouldn't budge.

"We'll never be able to clear all these rocks away," he said, the implications just beginning to dawn on him.

"Nope, never," Clay agreed, expressionless.

"Which means we can't get out."

"Yup."

"Which means we're stuck here forever," said Brett, who was getting more and more alarmed by the second.

"Yup," Clay repeated.

"Which means we're going to die down here after all!"

"Yup."

"Yup!? That's it?! You're not going to tell me we can at least try to move the rocks or something?"

Clay looked at Brett, then back at the pile of rocks. There was no doubt the situation was bleak. Worse than bleak. He had been so concerned about the dragon's fate, he had forgotten to worry about his own.

"We can try to move them," he said. "Won't do any good."

"Then maybe there's another way out?" Brett pressed.

Clay shook his head. "I don't see one."

"Can't you at least be upset about it?"

"I am. I just—"

"What? Don't care?" said Brett, exasperated. "I mean, sorry if you detect a note of panic in my voice, Mr. Cool Guy, but personally, I'd rather not die down here. I happen to have a very different plan for my death that involves a few delectable items of the food variety, such as—"

Clay smiled sardonically. "Those Jell-O parfaits?"

"Yes! Those Jell-O parfaits, and then—"

"Shh." Clay put his finger to his lips. "Did you hear that?"

"What?"

"I thought I heard somebody calling my name."

"I didn't hear anything...."

They looked around the cave. There was no sign of anyone else—or of any activity at all.

"Could it be Ariella, like, mentally calling you?" Brett suggested tentatively.

Clay tilted his head, considering. "Nah, the voice was coming from somewhere in this cave. And, anyway, Ariella must already be out of the mountain by now."

"Wait a second!" said Brett, getting excited. "Think. There *has* to be another way out of here. How did Ariella get in, in the first place? Not through the tunnel. They had to bomb the tunnel to make it big enough for a dragon, right? And if there's another way in, then..."

"There's another way out," said Clay, catching on. "I like your thinking."

"But where is it?" Brett anxiously scanned the cave walls.

Clay nodded to himself. "I know where."

"Well...?" Brett prompted.

"Up."

Brett glanced upward. His excitement vanished.

"Um, you're not talking about *that*, are you?"

There was one visible opening: a fissure in the ceiling. It was large—more than large enough for Clay and Brett, large enough for even a dragon—but it was about thirty feet high, and directly above the lava pit.

Beyond the fissure: darkness.

"Uh-huh."

"Seriously?"

"It's our only option," said Clay.

It was the way he'd flown out in his dream. That was why he felt sure it was the right way to go. Of course, that was the same dream in which he'd shot out of the volcano and rocketed into outer space. Maybe not the easiest dream to replicate.

"You're insane," said Brett, despairing once again. "We'll never get up there."

"I can help," said a muffled voice.

Brett turned around, startled. "Who said that!?"

"I'm down here, you idiots, behind the boulder on your right."

They looked down into the rubble behind the boulder, expecting to see one of Brett's father's men. Instead, it was Flint, immobile and covered with dust and soot. One of his legs and both of his arms were lodged under rocks. His torn, filthy backpack lay in front of his mouth. He tried to nudge it away with his chin.

"I said I can help—if you get me out of here," he said.

"Jeez. You okay?" said Clay. The fire-happy junior counselor was the closest thing Clay had to an enemy, but he didn't necessarily want to see Flint buried alive.

"Oh, yeah, never better," replied Flint. "You should try lying under ten tons of rock. It's a blast."

"Sorry for asking. Flint, this is Brett. Brett, meet Flint."

"Pleased to meet you," said Brett. "Guess, um, I won't try to shake your hand?"

"Ha-ha." Flint peered up at Brett through dusty eyelashes. "You're the missing guy?"

Brett nodded. "Well...I was."

"I didn't think you were real."

"That's okay. My dad didn't, either."

"I know what you mean." Flint started to laugh, then grimaced in pain. "Come on, dudes. Get these rocks off me. I have ropes and stuff, but you guys won't be able to use them by yourselves. That climb out of here is going to be hella hard."

Clay shook his head scornfully. "Like we would just leave you there if you couldn't help us? Not everyone's as much of a tool as you are."

"Easy to call me names when I can't move," said Flint, spitting dust out of his mouth.

Clay turned to Brett. "Come on."

They bent down and started pushing rocks away from Flint, until there was just one left—a big rock sitting on his leg.

They tried to push it off.

"Ow! You trying to kill me?" Flint complained. "Stop pushing. Just pick it up...gently!"

The rock was heavy, but together Brett and Clay lifted it off Flint's leg and dropped it onto the ground next to him. There was a collective sigh of relief.

"Can you move it?" Brett asked.

Flint rolled his leg a little. "Yeah, it's fine—I'm fine," he said, even though it was pretty obvious that he wasn't.

Wincing, he stood up. He looked like he'd been through a war, bloodied and bruised all over.

"What were you doing down here, anyway?" Clay asked him suspiciously.

"Trying to stop those guys. Same as you."

Clay's eyes narrowed. "Oh yeah? I thought maybe you were helping them."

Ignoring Clay, Flint leaned over to pick up his backpack, and—

"Aaah!"

—cried out. "Just a sore muscle," he said quickly. "No big deal."

"Remember Leira and me saw you talking on the phone?" said Clay. "You weren't telling them where to go?"

"Maybe I was." Flint pulled a climbing rope out of his backpack and started uncoiling it. "And maybe I changed my mind."

"*Maybe* you changed your mind?" Clay shook his head, trying to control his rage. "The coolest, raddest, most awesome creature in the world—probably the last one in the world—is gone. Because of *you*—"

"And you did such an awesome job protecting it, huh?" said Flint, tying a grappling hook to the end of the rope.

"Man, you are such a—"

"Can you two not fight right now?" Brett interjected anxiously. "It's time to get out of here."

"Just what I was thinking," said Flint. "Now, watch and learn, boys—"

With more than a touch of his old swagger, he began twirling the rope high above his head. If the movement caused him pain, he didn't show it. The shiny hook reflected the orange glow of the lava, and as he twirled the rope faster and faster—faster than seemed humanly possible—Clay and Brett watched the hook blur into a perfect glowing circle.

Murmuring a few words to himself, Flint finally released the rope; the hook end flew straight into the gap in the cave ceiling and locked onto the rocks inside. It would have been an astonishingly precise hit even for someone who wasn't injured. A hole in one.

Brett shook his head in wonder. "How did you—?"

"How else are we supposed to get up there," said Flint, tugging on the rope to make sure it was secure.

"Yeah, but that was—"

Flint laughed. "Magic?"

Oh well, Clay thought. At least it was somebody else who'd said it, not him.

"Brett doesn't know about you," he explained to Flint. "Or the camp or anything."

"Huh? Oh. Oops." Flint laughed again. "Well, that was nothing. Check this out—"

Making a gun with his hand, he shot a series of bright white flares out of his fingertip. They died out only after they'd entered the gap in the ceiling and illuminated the craggy space above.

"Now we know where we're going," said Flint with a grin.

A moment later, they were off. And up.

Even Brett, who had terrible memories of trying to climb ropes in gym class, was pleasantly surprised to find himself rappelling out of the lava cave as if he'd been doing it all his life. Of course, it was a little alarming to see the rope burn away behind him like an oversized candlewick, but he tried not to look.

Things got much trickier when they got through the fissure into the cave above.

Flint had shot more flares out of his finger to light up the space—these flares lingered much longer than the previous ones—and they could see that while the cave was not very wide, it was very, very tall.

In front of our heroes: forty feet of near-sheer rock. The only opening: at the top.

"Now what?" Brett asked. "No way are we going up that rock."

Without an-
swering, Flint tied
the three of them
together with another
rope and started doing
just that.

Swallowing, Clay and Brett followed.

It was slow going, and very nerve-racking, but it wasn't quite as difficult as they had expected. That is to say, it wasn't impossible. *When* they imitated Flint's movements.

Whenever Clay tried to find his own spots to hold, he noticed that the rock was cold and slippery in his hand; and at one terrifying moment, he actually started to fall—only to be stopped by Flint's rope. In contrast, whenever he grasped a handhold that Flint had established for them, the rock was almost searingly hot, but Clay's grip held firm, and he was able to keep ascending. It was as if Flint were melting the rock just enough to make it mold to their fingers.

Brett, who was following close behind Clay, seemed to notice the same thing. "I didn't think I was such a good climber," he said, breathless with exertion but somehow managing to keep up. "And I'm really not, am I?"

"Let's just say I wouldn't count on being able to do this again," said Clay. "At least not without Flint leading the way."

About twelve feet above them, Flint was pulling himself up the last portion of the rock face. There was nothing overtly magical about what he was doing, but every once in a while, when his hand touched rock, sparks would fly from his fingers, as if they were knives on a grindstone.

"Does everyone at your camp have talents like he does?" Brett asked.

"Like Flint? Not exactly," said Clay. "Some of us don't have much talent at all."

It was clear that he meant himself.

"*You?* You talk to dragons!" said Brett, incredulous. "I would call that a talent."

Clay shook his head. "A lot of good it does now that the dragon's gone."

His anger rising again, he looked up at Flint.

"Hey, how did you hook up with those guys, anyway?" he called out, as if they'd just been talking about it. "Brett's dad and everyone."

"It wasn't his dad," Flint called back. "It was this woman his girlfriend works for. . . . Come on, pick up the pace!"

Clay found Flint waiting for them on a blissfully wide ledge. His expression was impatient, but Clay suspected that he needed the rest. His injuries were catching up with him.

"What woman?" asked Brett, hoisting himself up to join them.

"I don't really know anything about her," said Flint. "Not even her name."

Clay frowned. "But you met her?"

"When I was eleven. I was back in court for lighting a fire—just a few flames in a toilet, but they acted like I tried to burn down the whole school."

"People tend to take fire seriously," Brett noted. "It's a thing."

"Yeah? What about the whole you-need-fire-to-have-a-civilization thing?" retorted Flint.

"You were trying to build a civilization in a toilet?" said Brett.

Flint glared. "Up yours."

Clay smirked.

Flint started to walk along the ledge toward what looked like the entrance to another tunnel. Far below was the opening into the lava cave. Clay and Brett followed, trying not to look down.

"Anyway, all the shrinky-dinks testified that I was a nut job," said Flint. "And they were ready to lock me up, when this woman arrives like a freaking fairy godmother or something. Most beautiful woman I ever saw, but kind of spooky. Her face never moved, and she always wore these white gloves.... She told me I wasn't crazy; I was special."

"You're pretty special, all right," said Clay.

Brett laughed.

"You guys better watch it," said Flint angrily. "I'm the one leading you out of here, remember?"

"Don't worry," said Brett. "We remember."

"So then what happened?" asked Clay. Flint's description of the white-gloved woman had sounded familiar to him; he wasn't sure why.

"Then, next thing I know, she works some kind of voodoo, the charges against me are dropped, and I'm being shipped off to Earth Ranch. *Learn everything you can*, she says. *And don't ever mention me.* For three years, those were my only instructions. But this summer she gives me the phone and says, *They trust you now. Start looking. Look everywhere. You'll know it when you see it.* And when I saw the dragon paintings, I knew—"

"You were a spy," said Clay. "A traitor."

"So? I'm supposed to feel bad about it?" Flint scoffed. "Mr. B, Buzz, everybody—they all make great speeches about the Other Side and the sacredness of magic and all that, but they aren't protecting magic; they're just scared of it."

"Maybe," said Clay. "Or maybe they know what they're talking about."

"Whatever. This woman, she says there are no rules when it comes to magic, because magic *is* the breaking of rules."

It was indeed the entrance to another tunnel that they'd seen, but a very steep and very narrow tunnel. There was no other way to go, however, so Flint shot a few more flares into it, and in they went.

"If she's so smart, what made you change your mind?" Clay asked, keeping pace with him now. "Feeling guilty?"

"As if!" Flint snorted. "She said they would make me a Dragon Tamer, but she lied."

"Nobody can make you a Dragon Tamer," said Clay. "You are one or you aren't."

Flint stopped and pointed at Clay. "So you took the book after all! I knew it."

"What do you care?" said Clay. "You'll never see a dragon again anyway."

"Maybe *you* won't," said Flint.

"Come on, face it, she's done with you. And it serves you right."

Flint's eyes burned. "Nobody's done with me until I say they are. The Midnight Sun will be sorry they ever met me."

"The Midnight Sun?" An unexpected chill traveled up Clay's spine.

Flint nodded, and started walking again. "That's their group. International secret society or some junk like that. Bunch of creeps in white gloves. I only ever heard the name once, but I never forgot."

The Midnight Sun.

When Clay was little, he had heard his brother talk about the Midnight Sun a few times with his friend Cass—always in hushed tones, and only when he thought Clay wasn't listening. As a rule, Max-Ernest was compulsively talkative. The Midnight Sun must have scared him quite a bit for him to stay so quiet about it.

Could it be the same Midnight Sun that had sent Flint to Earth Ranch and that was now in possession of Ariella? Was that why the description of the white-gloved woman had sounded so familiar?

"What does the Midnight Sun want with a dragon?" he asked.

"My dad said they were taking the dragon to a sanctuary," Brett volunteered.

"Yeah, that's what they call it." Flint's laugh was more of a wheeze. He didn't sound good. Or look good. "It's where they're going to breed their army."

"Army?" Brett and Clay repeated together.

"Yeah, an army of dragons, they said. Hundreds of 'em."

"What are they going to do with hundreds of dragons?" Clay tried to imagine it. A single dragon had seemed difficult enough to manage. He thought of the *Secrets of the Occulta Draco*. What did the book say? *He who has power over dragons has power over us all.*

"Whatever they think they're going to do, they'll do it over my dead body," said Flint. "I'm not letting them take that dragon without a fight."

"Oh yeah? How are you gonna stop them?" said Clay.

"I thought you read the book. If you master the Occulta Draco, you can do anything."

"But you have to have a dragon for that," said Clay. "And the only dragon around has gotta be on that boat by now. For all we know, they're already sailing for the Sahara or wherever-the-heck."

"Then we'll just have to move faster, won't we?" said Flint.

The tunnel was almost level now, and Flint took the opportunity to increase his speed.

"Are you serious?" Clay asked, struggling to keep up. "You really want to go after them?"

Was it possible his enemy was becoming an ally?

"You know it. Are you in?"

Clay hesitated.

"Yeah," he said finally, a little flame of hope flickering inside him. "I'm in."

"Cool. Shake?" Flint extended his hand, but when Clay reached for it, Flint pulled his hand away and mimed slicking back his hair.

"Oh, that's a new one," said Clay, but he laughed anyway.

"Look!" said Brett, catching up with them. "Is that sky?"

About fifty feet ahead there was an opening; the tunnel was coming to an end.

"I think so," said Clay, excitedly striding toward it. "Flint—we going fast enough for you now?"

There was no answer.

"Flint?"

The other boys turned around. The talented teenager was lying on the ground behind them, the contents of his backpack strewn beside him. They rushed back.

"Jeez, you okay?" asked Clay.

"Does it look like I am?" said Flint, his eyes closed.

Brett scanned him for new injuries. "What happened? Is it your leg?"

"It's my everything."

Clay and Brett eyed each other. Their exit from the mountain was about to get a bit harder.

CHAPTER
SEVENTEEN

A CRASH LANDING

I knew there was a reason I kept this thing around, thought Captain Abad.

Holding her didgeridoo like a baseball bat (or maybe, since she was from Australia, I should say like a cricket bat), Captain Abad took a few practice swings.

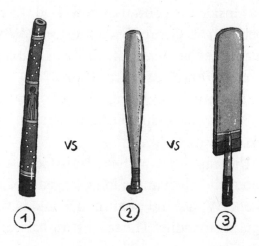

VS   VS

① ② ③

She didn't normally resort to shattering windows—she was a grown woman, after all, and a captain at that—and she couldn't help worrying that her precious didgeridoo might get scratched, but these were exceptional circumstances. The guard who'd been posted beneath her window all day had just left, presumably to go to the bathroom or call for a replacement, and she might not have another opportunity to break out of her quarters.

Ready to swing, the captain took one last look outside—then froze with her didgeridoo suspended over her shoulder. The guard had returned, and he was motioning to a helicopter that was hovering a mere thirty feet or so above the *Imperial Conquest*. Dangling from the helicopter was the rusty shipping container that she'd last seen occupied by a twelve-year-old boy who would later be pushed off the ship. She wondered what was inside the container now. Had the mysterious Operation St. George been a success? What prize was so valuable that a gang of criminals had commandeered an entire cruise ship to attain it?

The container was being lowered onto the ship's loading deck when, suddenly, it started swinging wildly in every direction.

As the captain watched, transfixed, the container door slid open and a long, jagged reptilian tail slipped out. What kind of animal would have such a tail? A giant crocodile? The tail swung back and forth like a whip, thwacking the sides of the container and causing it to jerk this way and that.

Outside the captain's window, people started screaming and running in every direction. The helicopter pilot tried to rectify the situation by pulling back from the ship, but that only made the container swing more violently. *SMASH!* The captain heard the container collide with the ship at a spot high above her, probably taking out the ship's radio antenna and radar equipment, by the sound of it. She shook her head in dismay. It would be that much harder to call for help once she escaped.

She figured that the container had become unhooked from the helicopter. But, no, there it was again a moment later, swinging into view, the strange tail still sticking out the door. As the container careened by her window, she caught a quick glimpse of the thing that was thrashing around inside. The captain's heart beat wildly in her chest, and she wondered for a moment if she were losing her grip on reality. The great beast's jaws were muzzled and its wings were bound, but there was no mistaking it for anything other than what it was. And yet—

—a dragon?!?

The captain considered herself a rational, scientifically minded person; she was not a fan of fairy tales and fantasy stories. On the other hand, part of being a scientist, as she understood it, was accepting empirical evidence when it was presented to you. You didn't simply deny the existence of a thing because it didn't 'fit into your theory of the universe; the existence of the thing meant that your theory of the universe was flawed. And a dragon—a real dragon—what an amazing discovery that would be! For a dragon, you might do far more than commandeer a cruise ship. You might travel to the ends of the earth. There was still enough of the adventurer in Captain Abad for her to feel more than a small tingle of romance at the sight of the ancient beast.

Here be dragons, it said on the old maps. Well, here be one at last.

Then—*CRASH!*—there were screams and the sound of shattering glass. The container had collided with the ship again, this time landing much nearer to the captain's quarters.

Wasting no more time, she took advantage of the noise and mayhem to smash her window open. As she leaned out and looked aft, she saw that the container had crashed into somebody's stateroom.* It had broken free from the helicopter and was now hanging off the stateroom's small balcony. The container hung there for a second longer; then there was a terrible creaking sound, and the balcony gave way.

---

* Aft MEANS IN THE DIRECTION OF THE STERN. DON'T REMEMBER WHAT STERN MEANS? PITY. DID YOU NOT READ THE FOOTNOTE ON PAGE 61?

The container smashed through two more balconies before coming to a crash landing on the deck below.

It is a terrible thing for a captain to watch her ship being destroyed, but Captain Abad's first thought was not for her ship but for her passengers. As far as she could tell, no one had been hurt. The screams she'd heard were screams of terror, not pain. The dragon, though—how had it fared in the fall? Now that the dragon was on her ship, she was responsible for it; it was her passenger.

Craning her neck, she could see the dragon standing half in and half out of the container. Its wings were still bound together, and at least one chain was still bolted to the container floor, but somewhere along the way the dragon's muzzle had come off.

The dragon looked upward, it eyes briefly meeting the captain's, and then let out a tremendous roar, sending a ball of fire high into the sky.

The captain was awestruck. And terrified. One more breath like that in the right direction and the entire ship could go up in flames.

The dragon was just raising its head again when it was shot with hundreds of darts. It staggered, then fell to the ground, chains hitting the container with a *clang*.

The captain didn't know whether she was more relieved for her ship or more furious for the dragon.

The intercom crackled, and in a moment Amber's cheerful, reassuring voice could be heard. "Ladies and gentlemen, please do not be alarmed. There has been an accident involving a shipping container, but it is now under control, and there have been no injuries reported. Some people are saying that they saw a giant lizard inside the container, but of course they saw no such thing. A coiled fire hose got loose, that is all. There was no swinging tail...."

Captain Abad shook her head. If anyone could get people to disbelieve their own eyes, it was Amber. But there was no time to worry about what the passengers thought. The captain had to reconquer the *Imperial Conquest* before it was too late.

Doing her best to avoid the broken glass, she climbed out the window and lowered herself to the deck below.

CHAPTER
EIGHTEEN

TITANIC MEETS GODZILLA

As an author, I regard my characters as my children. (Especially those who happen to be children.) In my eyes, they can do almost no wrong. Nonetheless, I am duty-bound to report the truth about them, and all in all, it hadn't been the Worms' finest hour. Nor Mira's. Nor even, I confess, Leira's.

From their mountaintop hiding place, they heard multiple explosions. They knew that all kinds of terrible things were happening inside the volcano, and they knew that their friend Clay was stuck right there in the middle of it.

And yet what did they do?

Nothing.

Even when the dragon was dragged out in chains and shoved like the world's biggest sack of potatoes into the shipping container, they only watched in horrified wonder. It was hard enough to comprehend that a mythical creature like a dragon might live and breathe like any other animal. And then that a beast so magical and mighty could be treated so ignobly!

For a moment, it had looked like the helicopter might be unable to lift the combined weight of the container and the dragon, and our friends were briefly hopeful that the dragon would get to stay on the island after all. But after a few false starts, the container was airborne, and the caged dragon was on its way.

In defense of my not-so-brave-acting characters, I will point out that there was no way they could have stopped the helicopter from where they were—at least no way that I can imagine. As for saving Clay, the only way into the mountain that they were aware of was guarded by at least twenty grown men and women, all well armed with firearms and explosives and who knew what else. In contrast, there were only five on the campers' side, none over the age of fourteen, and none of them armed.

Only when the sun started to go down did Leira, who, by virtue of being the first to know about the dragon, had become group leader, tell the others to stand up and get moving. By then Brett's father's crew had dispersed, and she felt reasonably confident that the campers were alone.

They were about to head down to see if there was still a way into the cave, when Jonah stopped his friends and pointed.

"Looks who's there!"

Three people were silhouetted high up on the mountain. It was clear from their shapes and sizes that Clay, Brett, and Flint had all made it out of the volcano alive.

Alive—but in Flint's case, barely so.

With Clay and Brett propping him up from behind, Flint had just managed to walk the last twenty feet of the tunnel. The walk took all his strength, and as soon as he was in the open air, he collapsed to the ground again, his face sweaty and pale.

"Gotta get up," he mumbled to himself. "Gotta get..."

But when he tried to push himself back up, he couldn't.

"Dude. Stop," said Clay. "We'll carry you."

"No, no, I'm okay," Flint said, gasping for breath. "I'll catch up. Go get the dragon!"

Clay and Brett looked at each other, then back at Flint.

"Sorry, man, but you are not okay," said Clay.

"Definitely not," agreed Brett. "Besides your collarbone, I'm guessing fractured rib, broken tibia, and a sprained ankle, to start. And then there are the internal organs...."

A moment later, Clay and Brett were doing their best to carry Flint down the mountain as promised—first carrying him over their shoulders, then holding his legs and arms, then carrying him over their shoulders again. Nothing quite worked. Eventually, they had to start dragging him.

"Hope we're not hurting you too much," said Brett.

Flint looked at him through heavy-lidded eyes. He seemed about to make a sarcastic rejoinder, but the effort to speak was too much.

After the other campers had joined them, and Brett had been introduced to everyone, and all of them had expressed their amazement about the events of the day, an argument erupted about what to do with Flint. The campers had so little love for the pyromaniac junior counselor that there were several half-serious jokes about leaving him to fend for himself, just as he had suggested.

"He left you on the beach, remember?" said Kwan to Clay. "Turnabout is fair play and all that."

"Yeah, but *I* could walk by myself," said Clay. "C'mon. There has to be somewhere safe we can put him."

"Nowhere is safe for Flint if he doesn't get some medical help," said Leira.

"But Nurse Cora is locked in the library with everybody else," Mira pointed out.

"Then that's where we have to take him," said Clay.

And let's make it fast, he thought.

Far out in the ocean, he could see the *Imperial Conquest*. It looked as though it was still anchored. But for how long? He had to get on the ship before it sailed too far away. He owed it to Flint. And, more important, to Ariella.

In groups of three, the campers took turns carrying Flint, walking close together in single file with him over their right shoulders, like lumber at a construction site. Somehow, they managed to get him to the vicinity of the library without dropping him—and without seeing anyone from Brett's father's crew.

But at the library tower two of the armed men were still standing watch. Evidently, Brett's father still feared that someone would try to stop him.

And someone will, thought Clay.

"Perfect," said Kwan, gritting his teeth. "Now what?"

"No worries, I've got this," said Pablo. "Clay, give me a hand, bro—"

Two minutes later, this is what you would have seen if you were one of the men guarding the library: a teenage boy, Flint, stumbling toward them, waving and yelling, "Take me inside! I need to see Nurse

Cora!" Until he fell to the ground, unconscious, and very possibly dead.

If, however, you had witnessed the same event from a vantage point behind Flint, you would have seen something else entirely: Clay and Pablo propping him up while Clay shouted Flint's lines and Pablo manipulated Flint's hands and arms like a puppet's. As soon as he dropped to the ground, they dived under a bush. Just in time to escape the guards' notice.

Hidden by the shrubbery, the campers watched as the guards walked over and prodded Flint with their rifles. They appeared to be arguing about what to do with him, and for a moment Flint's fate was uncertain, but finally the guards lifted Flint by the arms and dragged him into the library.

The kids high-fived one another. Success!

"It's just like a crime show," whispered Mira. "You know, when the bad guys are too afraid the police will catch them if they walk into a hospital, so they leave somebody bleeding on the hospital steps instead?"

"I thought we were the good guys," said Jonah.

"We are. And now we're going to prove it," said Clay. He looked at his friends. "Who here knows how to get on that boat?"

"You mean the cruise ship—why?" said Kwan.

"Yeah, why?" echoed Pablo. "Those things are just

giant floating displays of everything that's wrong with the world...mass consumerism...destruction of the ecosystem...old people..."

"Wait till you try the Jell-O parfaits before you dis cruise ships," said Brett. (It sounded as though he were joking, but you and I know that he wasn't. Or wasn't quite.) "And by the way, you'll be old, too, someday."

Leira sized up Brett and Clay. "You guys want to go after that dragon, don't you? Nice idea, but—"

"Totally cray cray?" volunteered her sister.

"I was going to say a total disaster in the making," said Leira. "But, sure, cray cray works, too."

"They're trying to build a dragon army; and if they do, trust me, it *will* be a total disaster," said Clay, thinking again of the *Secrets of the Occulta Draco. He who has power over dragons has power over us all.*

"Don't you need, you know, two dragons to make more dragons?" said Kwan.

"Maybe they're going to clone it," said Brett.

"Either way, Clay's right. It sounds bad," said Leira.

"And who knows what they're going to do to the dragon in the meantime!" said Clay. "We have to save Ariella from those guys."

"Ariella? That's the dragon's name?" said Jonah. "Sweet."

Pablo frowned. "Do you mean like *sweet* sweet,

or like sarcastic sweet, or like *Man, your ride is sweet sweet?*"

Jonah shrugged. "All of the above?"

"Question," said Kwan. "How're you going to save your dragon when people are guarding it with guns? And it's on a ship with thousands of people that's going to take off at any moment, if it hasn't already? Sorry, but my life is worth more to me than some magical fantasy animal that I didn't even know existed until two hours ago. I mean, sure, I played Dungeons and Dragons a few times, but..."

"Are you finished?" asked Jonah. "Because there's another possibility you're not thinking about. What if the dragon escapes on its own?"

"Yeah, so?" said Kwan. "Then it's all good, right?"

"No. Think about it—the dragon breathes fire, right? If it escapes, it could torch everyone on board." Jonah closed his eyes, seeing the scene in his mind. "Even if the dragon didn't do it on purpose, it could burn the whole ship. We're talking *Titanic* times ten."

"Or maybe *Titanic* meets *Godzilla*," Mira reflected morbidly.

Pablo laughed. "I'd like to see that."

"You're deranged," said Leira.

"True. That could all happen—full-on Dragon-maggedon," said Kwan. "But it could happen if we're the ones who free the dragon, too. The difference is, if we're there, we'll be the first ones to get toasted."

"You don't understand," said Brett. "The dragon won't hurt anyone if Clay is there. He's Ariella's friend."

"Friend?"

"Not really," said Clay quickly. "But yeah, kinda."

Leira looked at him. "You really think you can keep that dragon from burning the ship?"

Clay smiled weakly. It was true that Ariella seemed to like him—in a dragon sort of way—but that didn't mean the creature would be inclined to listen to him. Unless—

"No problem," he said. "I just have to do a little reading first—"

Flint had sounded very confident about the power of the Occulta Draco. Clay only hoped Flint was right.

"Oh, don't worry," said Kwan sarcastically. "There's plenty of time for reading. You just sit down with a book while the rest of us swim across the ocean, hijack a giant cruise ship, get shot by armed thugs, and then get eaten by a dragon."

"So you're saying you're in?" Clay asked.

It had only been a short while since Flint asked him the same question.

Kwan sighed. "Yeah, I'm in. I'm always in."

"Cool."

"Fantastic—I can't wait to see all you magic kids in action," said Brett. "But did I miss something, or have we still not figured out how we're getting across the ocean? Is there maybe a boat, for instance? Because I'm not swimming again."

"Who says we have to go by water?" said Leira, staring into the near distance.

The others followed her gaze.

Mr. B's teepee was still hiding behind the boulder near the library, floating a few inches off the ground. It seemed to be bouncing slightly, as if it had a case of the jitters.

As if it knew it was about to go on a dangerous journey.

Despite all that I have just written, there comes a time when every Dragon Tamer needs to convince a dragon to do something the dragon does not want to do—even if it is simply to fly home rather than burn down a village.

How do you persuade a beast that is so much older, wiser, bigger, and stronger than you are to do something contrary to its will? The answer to that question, young Tamer, lies at the heart of the Occulta Draco, the arcane body of knowledge that I will endeavor to pass on to you now. . . .

CHAPTER
NINETEEN

THE VERY TIPPY TEEPEE

Probably, it wasn't necessary for Leira to have snuck up on the teepee. Yes, the teepee bent away from her when she came near, but it didn't fly away altogether, as it might have. She grabbed one of the poles and held on tight as if the teepee were a wild horse, but it only pulled slightly, seemingly resigned to welcoming the motley crew of passengers.

"Do you think it will hold all of us?" asked Pablo, looking from his friends to the tattered canvas structure floating in front of them. "I mean, that's a lot of weight for a teepee to fly with."

Jonah laughed. "Any weight is a lot of weight for a teepee to fly with."

"Mira can stay behind," suggested Leira. "Then we'll be one less."

"What? I will not," said Mira.

"It's just because I love you and I want you to be safe."

Mira gritted her teeth, furious. "That's so not the reason and you know it!"

"Is so."

"Is not!"

They glared at each other, continuing their fight in silence.

The boys looked knowingly at Clay. It seemed obvious that he was the source of the sisterly disagreement.

"You really gonna let them fight over you like this?" Kwan whispered.

Clay shrugged, horribly embarrassed. The last thing he wanted to do was intervene, but they weren't going to get anywhere until Leira and Mira made peace.

He forced himself to speak. "It's okay. We can all hang out as much as you want later," he said, avoiding their eyes. "You don't have to fight about it."

Mira looked at him. Leira looked at him. There was an awkward silence.

Then both sisters started giggling. Then laughing. Then full out-and-out guffawing.

"You thought we were fighting over *you*?!" said Leira.

"Why would we ever—" said Mira. "Wait, oh no, you didn't think we had crushes on you, did you?"

Leira stared. "That's . . . I can't even—"

"You did, didn't you?!"

The truth was evident in Clay's blushing face.

Mira shook her head in exaggerated amazement. "O-M-G. You did! You thought we had crushes on you."

They laughed harder and harder until they both were doubled over.

"I don't know—I didn't really—it's just—" Clay stammered. "That's what they said." He pointed lamely at their friends.

Mira shook her head in disgust. "So you guys don't think girls have anything to fight about besides a boy?"

Leira pointed to Jonah. "You of all people should know better. You have two moms! They're going to be so mad when I tell them how sexist you are."

"Please don't," said Jonah nervously.

"So, what were you guys really fighting about, then?" said Clay, still unable to look them in the eye.

"I'll tell you what we've been fighting about— *her,*" said Mira, indicating her sister. "She never includes me in any of the fun stuff."

"You mean the dangerous stuff," said Leira.

"Same difference," said Mira. "Just because I like to wear dresses, you think I'm useless and can't be trusted. You're as bad as the boys are!"

"That is so not true!"

"Fine, then let me go with you! No, forget that. I mean, *watch* me go with you."

"Fine. I'm not stopping you."

"Fine," said Mira.

She stepped into the teepee—then promptly fell on her face.

As did all the others as soon as they got inside. The teepee was so tippy it was nearly impossible for anyone to stand up.

In other respects, Mr. Bailey's mobile summer home was surprisingly accommodating; it proved to be much bigger on the inside than it appeared from the outside, and despite the added weight, it had no trouble rising in the air after everyone had settled in.

Navigation was another matter.

Clay had been in the teepee only once before— when Mr. Bailey flew him over Earth Ranch and introduced him to the concept of the Other Side— but that was one more time than the others had been in the teepee, so it fell to him to steer the unlikely canvas aircraft. Just as he remembered, there was a campfire stove in the middle that filled the teepee with warm air in the manner of a hot-air balloon, and there were ropes and pulleys that adjusted the sides of the teepee as if they were sails on a sailboat. The problem was that whenever he pulled on a rope, too much hot air was released and the teepee started to plummet. And when he refilled it with hot air, the sides of the teepee ballooned outward and no longer caught the wind the way they were supposed to.

After a couple of heart-stopping drops and a few dizzying spins, Clay thought he was maybe, possibly, perhaps beginning to have a handle on steering the teepee. But then, checking on the stove, he accidentally let a rope slip out of his hands and—

"Aaaaaaah!"

—the teepee turned on its side. Screaming, they all slammed into one another and had to grab fistfuls of canvas to avoid sliding out.

Somehow, among the tangled limbs and flying debris, Clay found the loose rope and managed to pull on it. The teepee righted itself just in time.

"Well, that was fun!" said Mira, determinedly cheerful, though it was clear from her sweaty forehead that she'd been as frightened as everyone else. "Gee, sis, you look kind of ill. Not letting a little shake get to you, are you?"

"The only thing getting to me is you," her sister grumbled.

"Maybe if I stand, it'll be better?" said Clay when he could at last catch a breath.

Kwan snorted. "Anything would be better."

As I've already noted, standing was very difficult. But Clay had an innate sense of balance from his years of skateboarding, and after a couple of false starts, he was able to remain standing. This turned out to be the trick to successfully steering the teepee. Clay had better access to the ropes, and he could rely on his skateboarder instincts to help keep the teepee steady.

A smile crept onto his face. "You know, this thing is actually kinda awesome."

"Just don't get too confident!" warned Leira. "Stay scared so you pay attention to what you're doing."

"So what's our plan?" Pablo asked.

"You mean the plan of how seven kids are going to raid a giant cruise ship and spring a fire-breathing dragon that's caged in a shipping container and protected by dozens of armed guards?" said Kwan. "That plan?"

"Yeah," said Pablo. "That plan."

Kwan shrugged. "No idea. Clay is the captain today, not me, in case you haven't noticed."

They all looked at Clay. He looked back at them.

Okay, he thought, I can do this. I *have* to do this.

"Brett, when you saw the container on the ship, where was it?" he asked. "You think they'll put it back there—with the dragon in it, I mean?"

Brett cleared his throat. (He wasn't normally so nervous about speaking. Then again, he wasn't normally listened to.) "Probably—I doubt they'd leave it out on the deck for everyone to see. It was in this big cargo-holding area in the middle of the ship. The problem is, to get in there, you need an all-access ID card."

"Yeah, that's where the container is—in the cargo hold," murmured Jonah, his eyes closed.

Brett stared at him. "Does he have X-ray vision, or does he see into the future?"

"I don't know," said Clay. "Both?"

Brett shook his head. "You're all like superheroes—it's ridiculous! When I get home, I'm getting you a TV deal."

"No!" the others said in chorus.

"Everything here is on the down low, remember?" said Pablo.

Jonah nodded. "Earth Ranch, magic, it's all secret."

Brett shrugged. "Suit yourselves."

Kwan scratched his head. "Really? You think we could do TV? How much cash do you think we'd get?"

Leira poked him. "Kwan!"

"Kidding!" said Kwan. "Sorry. Jeez, can't a man dream a little?"

Pablo snapped his fingers at them. "Can we be serious for a second, guys?" He turned to Brett. "So where do we get that all-access pass?"

"I had one, but it's at the bottom of the ocean now, which isn't very helpful, is it?" said Brett. "Let's see...I know some of the ship security staff have them."

"Perf," said Leira. "Just get me near one of those guys, and I'll take it from there."

Brett nodded. "I think I can do that."

"Okay," said Kwan. "Say we get that pass, and we get into the cargo hold, and say the container's there, and let's even say the dragon is there—then what happens?"

Silence. Nobody had an answer.

"How about we just wing it?" said Clay finally. "I have a feeling that once I'm in the room with Ariella—well, I just think I'll know what to do."

The book was in his backpack, but when was he going to have time to read it?

"Okay, then, that settles it," said Leira. "We'll wing it."

"Awesome," said Pablo.

"Cool," agreed Jonah.

"I love improv!" said Mira. "That's when the best stuff happens."

Kwan shrugged. "I guess it's unanimous. Improv it is."

The campers had long suspected that the comings and goings of the vog on Price Island were not wholly accidents of nature but rather responses to spells laid years ago. Often the vog seemed to descend for a specific reason—when something was on the verge of being found that wasn't supposed to be found, for example. Or, like today, when someone had need of the vog for cover.

Almost as soon as they'd boarded the teepee,

a thick layer of vog had started rolling in, as if in answer to their request. Clay had never before been so grateful for the gray, smoky air. Even with a dragon on board the cruise ship, a flying teepee was bound to attract attention. The vog would hide it... for a while.

And yet, flying in the vog meant flying blind.

Thankfully, they had Jonah to guide them.

"Slow down—the ship's right ahead of us," he said to Clay. "We want to get above it, right? Not overshoot it altogether."

"Seriously, you're like human radar," said Brett. "Are you sure you don't want to do TV?"

"What about the *ship's* radar?" Mira asked. "Won't it detect us?"

"I doubt they're on the lookout for teepees," said Leira. "For all they know, we're just some random bird flying by."

Mira laughed. "Yeah, a big, triangular random bird. I bet they see lots of those."

"Anyway, what are they going to do, shoot anti-aircraft missiles at us?" said Pablo. "You know I'm the most paranoid guy around, but seriously, it's a cruise ship, not a nuclear sub."

Before they knew it, they were hovering above the *Imperial Conquest*. They slowly circled the ship while Jonah peered into the vog, describing what he saw. Flying next to them, a flock of very determined seagulls kept careful watch over the ship's balconies, waiting for somebody to leave a half-eaten tray of food.

"Jeez, there are a lot of people down there," said Jonah. He shivered. "I don't know why, but I suddenly have a bad feeling about that ship."

Pablo raised an eyebrow. "Like it's going to make us sick?"

"Like it's going to make us *sink*," said Jonah darkly.

"Hey, Jonah, can you see the big door at the back of the ship—looks like a giant garage door?" said Brett. "That's where they load stuff into the cargo room."

"Yeah, I see it, but we can't go in that way," said Jonah as Clay maneuvered the teepee for him. "There's, like, a dozen of your dad's guys hanging around back there."

"Right. We go in the way I did before—through the kitchen," said Brett. "That big door is our way out."

"How're we going to land with so many people on deck?" said Leira. "That's the question."

"Don't you guys have invisibility cloaks or something?" asked Brett.

The others looked at him.

"Okay, guess not."

"What we need is a distraction," said Kwan. "Pablo, what you got?"

Pablo looked down at the ship. The vog was

starting to dissipate, and now they could see the passengers moving around. "See that swimming pool? Clay, I need you to get me straight over it.... Right. Now a little lower. But don't let anyone see us!"

"How can I control that?" said Clay.

"Just do it."

When he was satisfied that they were in the right position, Pablo reached into his pocket. "Watch this, dudes—"

He stuck his hand out of the teepee and poured a stream of powder down into the pool. For a second, nothing happened.

Then the pool started churning and foaming like an oversized Jacuzzi. Suddenly, it erupted in a big geyser that sprayed water fifty feet in the air and all over the Lido Deck. Everyone on the deck—passengers and crew alike—ran for cover.

"Wow, what did you put in there?" asked Mira.

Clay laughed. "Same thing he put in my drink this morning, I bet."

"But that's a swimming pool down there, not a glass of juice," said Leira.

Pablo grinned. "Okay, so maybe I mixed in a few more things to increase the effect."

CHAPTER
TWENTY

NOW YOU SEE IT,
NOW YOU DON'T

C lay parked the teepee behind the ship's giant climbing wall.

It was a secluded spot, but even so, he didn't want to risk leaving the teepee there for more than a minute. After they'd all disembarked, he set the camping stove burner to high and sent the teepee sailing up into the clouds. He had no idea how to retrieve it, but he had a feeling that if they were successful, they would find another way back to the island. And if they *weren't* successful, well, they might not be going back to the island at all.

They had made it aboard the ship; that was the main thing.

No longer erupting, the swimming pool was back to normal—minus about half its water. As dazed attendants refilled the pool and mopped the deck, impatient swimmers and sunbathers stood around, eating pizza and waiting for the pool to reopen.

"Now You See Him, Now You Don't!...And now you do! If you didn't catch the last magic show, you're in luck because there's another one in five minutes," said an upbeat male voice over the intercom. "Get yourself over to the Shooting Stars Nightclub and Casino for the show of a lifetime."

Immediately, people started heading indoors.

"Follow them," said Brett. "There will be a security guy with a pass there, for sure," he added to Leira in a whisper.

Spreading out in order not to call attention to themselves, the campers joined the crush of cruisers going downstairs. It was so crowded they didn't realize they'd reached the Shooting Stars Nightclub and Casino until they were right in front of it, part of the wide, chaotic queue assembled for the next magic show. Meanwhile, other passengers were exiting the nightclub. Alas, judging from the stray bits of conversation that the kids could overhear, these people weren't particularly happy with the show they had just seen.

"Is that what they're calling magic nowadays?" "My dog does a better job of making a rabbit disappear." "I'm telling you, he wouldn't last a day in Vegas!" "Does he think the sunglasses make him look cool?"

But perhaps it was just that the complainers were

louder than the happy customers. (You know how that is, right?) Swept up in the crowd, our friends were about to enter the nightclub when Brett was stopped by a man standing outside the door.

"Hey, aren't you—? What are you doing here?"

Uh-oh. It was one of Brett's father's men, now working as a bouncer for the nightclub.

"I don't know who you think I am," said Brett calmly. "But I'm a passenger on this ship, and my friends and I would like to see the magic show now."

They all nodded. "It's about to start!" "Let us in, please."

The bouncer looked at Brett suspiciously. "Are you sure you're not Brett junior? You better show me your ID right now or I'm taking you straight to Mr. Perry!" He nodded at Brett's friends. "That goes for all of you."

Before anybody else could respond, Mira yelled, "You're mean!" and started crying hysterically. As tears poured down her cheeks, years seemed to fall off her face.

In seconds, she became a much younger girl—a ten-year-old version of her true self. (And yet if you looked closely, her face hadn't changed at all, only her expression and her movements.)

"You're scaring me!" she shouted. "I want my mommy!"

As the bouncer stared, dumbfounded by her

transformation, other adults gathered around Mira protectively.

"What's wrong, sweetie?" "Did that man hurt you?"

"How dare you scare a little girl like that!" said an angry woman to the bouncer. "Who's your manager? I want to speak to your boss right away."

While the bouncer tried to defend himself, Mira cried even louder.

Taking advantage of the commotion, her friends ducked inside the nightclub.

"Did you get his card?" Kwan whispered to Leira.

She shook her head. "No time."

Kwan nodded. "Okay, I'm on it—"

As soon as they were gone, Mira stopped crying.

"Never mind, I feel better," she said, wiping away her tears. "I'm going to go find my mommy now."

She marched off in the direction the others had gone, only to be stopped by a crew member when she got to the roped-off casino area.

"Sorry, miss. The casino is eighteen and over only."

Mira tossed her long red hair out of her eyes and looked at the crew member. The ten-year-old had vanished; she now had the face of an adult woman.

"I know!" she said, laughing in a decidedly grown-up fashion. "Thank you for the compliment, but I'm twenty-seven years old."

"Oh, sorry, I thought—never mind," said the crew member, taken aback. "Please enter."

Mira found the others gathered around a blackjack table, where Kwan was already sitting behind a big pile of gambling tokens, or chips, as they are known.

"See, I can be helpful sometimes," Mira whispered in her sister's ear.

"Yeah, I guess all that practice fake-crying to get Dad's attention comes in handy now and then," said Leira.

Mira glared.

Leira smiled. "Okay, okay, it was cool what you did, I admit it."

On the table in front of Kwan was a jack of hearts and an eight of spades. "Hit me," he said, slapping the cards with his hand.

"Are you sure?" the dealer asked skeptically. "Usually people stand when they have eighteen."

"You bet I'm sure, Pretty Lady."

The dealer gave him a look. "You've got chutzpah, kid, I'll give you that. But if you call me that again, I'll have you out on your ear."*

She pulled a card from the "shoe" and put a three of clubs on the table.

---

* CHUTZPAH IS A YIDDISH WORD THAT MEANS, ROUGHLY, "GUMPTION" OR "BOLDNESS"; IT'S A WILLINGNESS TO DEFY EXPECTATION. BUT LIKE MOST YIDDISH WORDS AND PHRASES—SCHLEMIEL, SAY, OR MESHUGENER, OR EVEN OY VEY OR OY GEVALT!—THE WORD CHUTZPAH LOSES SOMETHING IN TRANSLATION. IT'S BEST TO REPEAT THE WORD ITSELF. EVEN IF YOU'RE NOT CERTAIN OF THE DEFINITION, YOU'RE SURE TO ENJOY PRONOUNCING IT.

Her eyes widened. 3 + 18 = 21. *Blackjack.*

Kwan grinned and pumped his fist. "How 'bout I call you Lady Luck instead?"

He was just gathering his chips into one big mound when he spied a burly man in a dark suit—a casino security officer—walking toward them.

Kwan winked at his friends. Bingo.

"How's it going?" asked the security officer when he reached the table. "Having fun?"

"Definitely," said Kwan. "It's going awesome! Look how much money I've already made!"

"Not counting cards, are you?"

"Why? What do you care?" Kwan scoffed. "We're not in Vegas."

"It's illegal wherever you are." The security officer frowned. "How old are you, anyway?"

While they were speaking, Leira had brushed casually against the security officer. She gave Kwan a thumbs-up, quickly flashed a shiny ID card, and then disappeared into the crowd.

"You know what?" said Kwan. "I changed my mind. I don't want to play anymore."

"Good," said the security officer, confused. "Then beat it."

"Will do!" said Kwan, jumping up.

"What's the fastest way to get in trouble at a casino?... Win!" he said to his friends as they headed out. "It's the only thing you're not allowed to do."

Leira rejoined them before they reached the exit. "Better not go out that way," she said. "Look—"

The bouncer was still standing by the door, watching people go in and out. Meanwhile, behind them, the security officer was standing in front of the casino area, arms crossed.

There was only one safe option: to walk deeper into the nightclub and sit down for the magic show.

They settled into their seats just as the magician walked onstage. He was now wearing his top hat, and he looked...better! Definitely better! Much, much better, really. Amber had seen to it that his suit was, well, slightly less rumpled, anyway. And with the stage lights lending their sparkle, and with the exhilaration of a live theatrical event putting a flush in his cheeks, I believe you could begin to see just how terribly handsome and dashing I—I mean *he!*—was beneath his sunglasses.

"Welcome to an evening of magic and mystery," he said with an engaging smile that would have won you over immediately if you'd been there, I promise. "I come to you from the exotic East...Hoboken, New Jersey."*

The audience laughed heartily at this hilarious joke. Or, to put it another way, they smiled uncomfortably at this somewhat awkward witticism. (What

---

* NOTE TO READERS: THE MAGICIAN WAS KIDDING. NEITHER MAX-ERNEST NOR HIS BROTHER, CLAY, EVER LIVED IN HOBOKEN. WHICH I'M SURE IS A VERY NICE PLACE AND SHOULD NEVER BE THE BUTT OF ANYONE'S JOKES.

can I say? I, er, Max-Ernest was feeling very anxious and perhaps not delivering his magician's patter with his usual aplomb.)

"For my first trick, I would like to introduce you to my assistant, Quiche."

Bowing slightly, the magician removed his hat— and revealed his pet rabbit sitting on his head.

At this charming visual joke, the audience laughed much louder, although I admit that a few of them might have thought that the rabbit was sitting there by accident. (It was not an accident; the magician had rehearsed this joke with his rabbit over and over to get it right, suffering even the occasional indignity of rabbit, shall we call them, pellets in his hair, not to mention more than a few scratches on his nose.) The magician played along by pretending to be surprised. Then, in his inimitably witty style, he performed a series of tricks so clever and inventive you wouldn't believe it if I described them to you. I will only tell you that at the end of these magnificent wonderments, the rabbit was again sitting atop the magician's head—but this time Quiche was wearing a miniature top hat on his own furry little cranium!

Well, what do you think of that?! Not only an astonishing feat, but I daresay an adorable one as well! Do you not agree?

Is it any wonder that after such a demanding, tour de force performance, the magician would get a little confused and distressed when suddenly a group of rambunctious kids in his audience all stood up and started shouting, "Fire! . . . Fire! . . . Fire!"

It was Brett's idea—whispered to the others—that they shout "Fire!" as a way of getting everyone to exit the room with them. What they needed was the cover of a crowd. Otherwise, the bouncer would have picked them off one by one as they left.

Unfortunately, before panic and mayhem could properly ensue, a young woman in a yellow evening dress ran up onstage, crying "False alarm! False alarm!"

"Oh no! It's Amber, my dad's fiancée," said Brett under his breath to Clay. He tried to hide his face behind his arm.

"Don't worry," Amber said to the audience, smiling her dazzling smile. "If there really were a fire, the alarm would go off, right? And the sprinklers in the ceiling would turn on. But you're all dry, aren't you? And thank goodness for that!"

Her reassurances worked; everyone sat down. Disappointed, Brett and his friends were forced to sit down, too.

But not before—for one short but significant second—the magician raised his sunglasses and looked at Clay with an expression that was a peculiar combination of surprise, pride, relief, disbelief, love, guilt, and a certain wry humor about the odd turns that life sometimes takes. At least I assume all those things were conveyed in the magician's expression; I know he felt them.

By the time Clay looked back at him, however, the magician's sunglasses were again resting on his nose and he was no longer looking Clay's way.

Clay stared at the back of the magician's head, wondering if it was possible.... He had not seen a magic show in the two years since his brother left. Or not a magic show of the bunny-in-hat variety. So of course he'd been thinking about his brother from the moment he sat down. But he figured he was only imagining the resemblance. It seemed too unlikely a coincidence that it should really be his brother standing onstage in front of him. Besides, his brother's suits were always wrinkled, and his hair was always sticking up. Max-Ernest was a mess; this magician seemed, well, a hair more put together.

Still, he was almost certain the magician had been looking his way. And why else would he single out Clay?

"Sorry about the interruption, darling," said Amber to the magician. "Please continue your fantastic show!"

He smiled. "Of course. And thank you for volunteering! Every magician likes a lovely young woman to assist with his tricks. And I have the perfect trick for you! Do you remember Gateway to the Invisible, Amber?" He gestured to a dark mirrored cabinet standing behind him. "These days I do a version called

Up in Smoke. But in honor of the island nearby, I think we should call it Lost in the Vog. How 'bout that?"

Amber stared at him: "I knew I knew you! You're—"

But before she could say his name, the magician waved his wand over his hat, and suddenly— "Abracadabra!"—the hat was on fire, and Amber was engulfed in a big puff of smoke.

When the smoke dissipated, she was gone.

"Huh. Where did she go?" said the magician, with the kind of satisfied smile that only comes when you disappear a lifelong enemy.

He held up the flaming hat. "Oh no! It looks like there really was a fire all along! Everybody, run! Now! Get out of here before it's too late! Fire! Fire!"

He leaned down and whispered to his rabbit. "Sorry about the hat. We'll get it patched."

As the panicked audience started to leave, the kids looked at one another in confusion.

"That's not a real fire, just an act..." said Pablo.

"Why is he helping us like this?" asked Leira.

Because he's my brother, Clay thought.

It had to be Max-Ernest. It was the only explanation.

"I dunno what his deal is," said Kwan. "But don't look a gift horse and all that—let's bail."

As the group ran out, now protected by the crowd, Clay glanced back at the magician, who was looking at him again from behind his sunglasses.

Clay wanted to run over and hug him. Or hit

him. He wasn't sure which. Now that he was sure it was his brother, the old anger was returning in force. Maybe Max-Ernest had gotten rid of Amber for them, but his brother had also abandoned him. He'd only contacted Clay once in two years. And now he didn't even have the courage to say hello?

Clay was about to go confront Max-Ernest when Leira tugged on his sleeve. "C'mon, there's no time to dawdle! If we want to save Ariella, we have to run!"

He ran.

CHAPTER
TWENTY-ONE

ESCAPE ROUTINE

It didn't take Amber more than three minutes to escape from the old trick cabinet, but they were three long, long minutes in which she was forced to relive a terrible humiliation of her early teen years.

By the time she was free, Max-Ernest was gone, and she was very, very angry.

If only she'd recognized him a minute earlier, she could have had him dragged offstage by his ears and fed him to the dragon! Better yet, she could have thrown Max-Ernest into the brig with that moralistic sourpuss Captain Abad. Ha. He would die of boredom! Instead, Amber thought, she was going to have to hunt everywhere on the boat for him.

The idea that her nerdy middle school nemesis had returned after so many years to be a fly in the ointment of her life once again—ugh, it was enough to make her break out in hives!

She should have known he'd still be working with that wacky group of do-gooder crackpots, the Terces Society. (It spells *secret* backward—how obvious can you get? And those poor pathetic souls thought they were so clever!) Why else would Max-Ernest be on the ship if not for them? Funny, in the old days, when she had first learned of the Terces Society and their enemies, the Midnight Sun, all the players had loomed so large in her imagination. How harmless everyone appeared now in retrospect! Not just Max-Ernest and that crazy, pointy-eared friend of his, Cassandra, but also Yo-Yoji (why did she ever think he was so cool?) and that kooky old magician—what was his name?—Pietro. Max-Ernest certainly seemed to be following in Pietro's dilapidated footsteps, didn't he?

She could only imagine what Antoinette would say if she were to see Max-Ernest now. The French were cruelly snobbish, very strict about their manners and customs, none more so than the *grande madame* Antoinette Mauvais; and there had been many times over the last ten years when Amber had regretted making herself Antoinette's ward. She knew she could never fully please the ancient French woman. Well, if Max-Ernest was the alternative, she was more than glad to have thrown in her lot with Ms. Mauvais and the Midnight Sun. And now Amber was a grown woman herself, free—or relatively free—to manage her own operations in her own way, with no one looking over her shoulder. Of course, Ms. Mauvais was always look-ing over Amber's shoulder—she was always looking over everyone's shoulder—but at least it was from afar....

How much did Max-Ernest know about the dragon, or about their plans for it, Amber wondered. Had he seen the habitat? Those were the questions of the moment. It didn't matter so much what he knew personally. She would see to it that he never interfered with her affairs again. But whatever he knew, others might know as well. Those kids in the audience, for example. Max-Ernest had helped them escape. Why? What were they up to? And why were they with Brett junior?

She knew that kid would be a problem as soon as she'd met him. Oh, why couldn't he have just drowned like everyone else who gets pushed off a ship!

"Now, now, Amber, don't turn into the evil stepmother," she chided herself. "You're the nice one, remember? You're Cinderella. You're Sleeping Beauty. You're Snow White..."

Okay, I'll move on. Amber is not our main character, and she deserves no more page space. Forgive me— she's just too much fun to write about. How often do you get to have total control over your enemy's brain?*

---

* IF MIND CONTROL SOUNDS APPEALING TO YOU, CONGRATULATIONS— YOU'RE WELL ON YOUR WAY TO BEING A WRITER!

Let's go back to a much more heroic and likable character, whose thoughts and actions I have a somewhat closer knowledge of: Brett, who was by now back in the Lido Deck Snack Shack kitchen.

The Jell-O parfaits were still there, just as beautiful and tempting as Brett remembered—but, alas, much fewer in number. With the ship stalled, maybe the parfaits were in greater demand than they had been before. Or maybe some other kid had discovered them and single-handedly eaten half the ship's parfait supply. Brett hadn't had a decent meal in days, and he would have loved nothing more than to dive into the parfaits, but he knew there wasn't time. Almost tearing up with regret, he forced himself to turn away.

"That's it," he said, pointing to the steel door beneath the red light.

Leira slid the security officer's ID card through the slot, then tried the door; it wouldn't open. She tried again.

"It's not working," she said, gritting her teeth with frustration. "Maybe he didn't have a high enough access level."

"Or maybe he already reported it stolen, and it was canceled," said Kwan.

"Just try again," said Clay, who was unwilling to believe they'd gotten this far only to have a bad card.

Leira slid the card through the slot again.

Click.

Everyone smiled.

They entered cautiously, not knowing what they'd find.

As far as Brett could tell, there were just as many live animals in the hold as before. But their mood had changed drastically. The animals cowered in their pens, huddled together, as far away as possible from the shipping container—and from the terrifying predator inside. Doubtless, this was the first dragon they'd ever come across, but they knew instinctively that they were meant to be its food.

Clay stepped up to the container, put his eye to one of the airholes, and was immediately enraged by what he saw.

Ariella, the most majestic of beasts, in a monstrous cage.

The muzzle was back on the dragon's mouth, and its arms and tail were locked in manacles, but it was awake and could turn its head just enough for its big golden eye to meet Clay's smaller brown one.

In this hard metal environment, the dragon's eye looked meltingly soft.

"Hi, Ariella," said Clay quietly. "It's going to be okay. We're going to get you out."

The dragon's response was characteristically prideful; translated into human speech, it was something like, *Nobody lets us out; we come out when we choose to come out, you pathetic little human.* But it was not nearly as harsh as that makes it sound.

The dragon, Clay sensed, was strangely at peace with its situation. Perhaps it was just tired of fighting, but Clay suspected that Ariella was taking the long view. He couldn't get over the feeling that the dragon had willingly been caught, or at least that the dragon had known what was going to happen. It was as though some predetermined script were being played out, and Ariella was only mildly interested in watching the action, having already seen the ending.

"Hey, you—step away from that cage!"

Clay wheeled around to see two men entering the room. They both had guns in their hands—pointed in his direction.

"All of you—stand in a row with your hands up!"

"Are you police?" asked Pablo. "Are we being arrested?"

"Never mind that—just be quiet!"

One of the men spoke into a walkie-talkie: "They're in here, just like you said they'd be."

He listened to a voice on the other end, his eyebrows raised in incredulity. "You're sure?... Okay, you got it, boss."

He turned to the other man. "She says to lock 'em in the cage with the dragon."

"Seriously?"

"Yep. Most secure place on the ship, she says."

His companion laughed. "She's got a point there.... All right, kids, if there's any funny business, I'm going to take that muzzle off the dragon as soon as I throw you in with it."

A few minutes later, the kids were all sitting on the cold steel floor of the container, trying not to be too alarmed by the terrible rumbling coming from somewhere in the dragon's stomach—and the terrible stench.

"It's like being in a car with my dog," Kwan whispered. "Only worse."

"What do you mean?" said Jonah.

"The farting. Duh. This dragon is lethal."

Kwan's friends glared at him. Nobody knew how much the dragon understood—or what would offend it.

"Don't worry," said Leira to the dragon. "He didn't mean it."

"Psst! Clay..." said a familiar voice.

Clay glanced up from *Secrets of the Occulta Draco*, which he had been reading like his life depended on it—because it very well might.

He saw an eye staring at him through one of the airholes. An eye remarkably like his own.

"What's the bad word?" said the voice.

"Max-Ernest!?"

It was his brother. *Bad word* was like a secret handshake they shared. Or had shared, in the days when they shared things like secret handshakes.

"Yep, it's me. Or my eyeball, anyway. It's great to see you."

"Yeah..."

There were so many things Clay had wanted to say to his brother over the past two years, but the only thing he could think to say at the moment was the obvious:

"What are you doing here? On the ship, I mean."

"You're not going to believe this," said Max-Ernest, "but actually, weirdly, why I'm here, it's just a coincidence, it doesn't have anything to do with you. How 'bout that? I mean, of course it has to do with you, in a way, it affects you, and right now, I'm right here in this exact place to see you, but—"

"You're on the ship for another reason?" Clay finished for him.

His brother was a man of words—many, many words—and sometimes you had to force him to come to the point.

"Right," said Max-Ernest, relieved. "I'm following some people, some bad people—"

"The Midnight Sun."

"Right," said Max-Ernest, a little surprised. "We know they're building something somewhere, something big, like a stadium or a coliseum or something. They call it—"

"The Sanctuary."

"Right," said Max-Ernest, a little more surprised. "And anything the Midnight Sun is putting that much effort into can't be good. Unfortunately, we don't know where it is, except that it's in a desert somewhere. I'm on this ship hoping they'll lead me to it. And then we can figure out what it's for—"

"I know what it's for," said Clay.

"You do?" said Max-Ernest, even more surprised than he'd been before.

"Uh-huh. Look—" Clay stepped back so his brother could see inside.

"What is that?!" Max-Ernest's one visible eye blinked in surprise.

"Oh, that?" said Clay blithely. "That's a dragon."

"A what?!"

"A dragon. You really didn't know?"

"Max-Ernest! How convenient to find you here!" sang a voice from across the cargo room.

"Uh-oh, it's Amber!" Max-Ernest whispered. "I'd better go."

Amber was flanked by two members of Brett's father's crew. They walked casually in the direction of the container.

"You're just going to leave us here?" said Clay, aghast.

"Oh, right!" Max-Ernest surreptitiously unlatched the container door. "Okay, when I slide the door open, everybody run."

"We're not going without the dragon," said Clay.

"What? Are you joking?" Max-Ernest looked from Clay and his friends to the dragon and back again. They were clearly very serious. "Fine, there's no time to argue."

He pulled an odd assortment of skeleton keys from his pocket.

"Here—these were Houdini's for his escape routines. My old mentor, Pietro, gave them to me. If any keys can unlock the dragon, these can. I'll try to distract the baddies—"

"Thanks," said Clay, but his brother had already turned away.

"Bye," Clay added.

"Yoo-hoo, Amber! Over here!" he could hear his brother saying.

A moment later, it was silent outside the container.

Clay looked back at the dragon. "Ready to get that muzzle off, Ariella?"

As the dragon craned its neck toward him, Clay examined the skeleton keys, trying to determine which was the most promising one. Each was more oddly shaped than the next.

"Oh, give those to a professional," said Leira, grabbing the keys from him.

CHAPTER
TWENTY-TWO

SUNK

I would like to tell you about the brave exploits that followed. How our heroic friends from Earth Ranch vanquished all their enemies in the service of freeing a dragon. But the truth is, when you have a dragon on your side—an unchained, un-muzzled dragon; a dragon that isn't being shot with hundreds of tranquilizer darts—escape isn't terribly difficult.

That doesn't mean there wasn't some collateral damage, however.

In order to make an exit route, Clay had had no choice but to encourage Ariella to burn a hole in the side of the hold. But perhaps the big, fiery exhale that burned the hole was a tad bigger and fierier than necessary. The plume of fire went all the way through to the room where the ship's water tanks were held and out the side of the ship.* As a result, one side of the ship caught on fire, and the other side started flooding with water.

A disaster? Most assuredly. But I submit that it could have been much worse. If a nuclear torpedo had hit the ship, for example, that would have been worse.

Once Ariella shot out of the hole in the ship's hull as if from a cannon, the dragon soared briefly upward, then dropped down onto the top of the climbing wall and spread its wings as if to declare victory over the paltry earthlings scurrying around the ship below.

From the bottom of the wall, our friends anxiously watched the beast. Would Ariella breathe yet more fire on the ship until it was nothing more than a pile of ash floating on the surface of the ocean? Or would the dragon stay where it was, guarding its spoils while the ship sank and people dropped helplessly into the water?

In the end, Ariella resisted any impulse to wreak vengeance on the ship's inhabitants. Instead, the dragon performed what might best be described as

---

* DID YOU KNOW THAT MOST OF THE DRINKING WATER ON CRUISE SHIPS IS PURIFIED SEAWATER? PERSONALLY, I FIND THIS FACT TO BE FASCINATING AND THE ONE SMALL ARGUMENT IN FAVOR OF CRUISE SHIPS. AS FRIGHTENING A PROSPECT AS IT IS, CRUISE-SHIP TECHNOLOGY MAY HOLD THE KEY TO A POST-APOCALYPTIC FUTURE THAT HAS US ALL LIVING IN ORBITING SPACECRAFT OR UNDERWATER PODS.

a magic trick. As everyone stared, Ariella dove down from the wall and glided over the deck and pool, passing right by our friends from Earth Ranch. Then the dragon rose again, spreading its wings wider and wider as it flew, until they seemed to fade away altogether and the creature was completely camouflaged against the darkening sky. It was as though the dragon had vanished into the air.

Straining his eyes, Brett could just make out the blurry outline of the dragon flapping its wings and lifting itself into the clouds.

But in a moment, the dragon had disappeared. Even to him.

He stared into the sky, happy and sad at once.

"Hey, Brett, where's Clay?"

Leira was tapping him on the shoulder. It was time to find a way off the ship. Before it sunk with them on it.

"Oh, he said he'd meet us back onshore," said Brett, a little smile on his lips. "He caught an early flight."

Leira followed his gaze into the clouds. Was Brett saying what she thought he was saying?

Was Clay responsible for the dragon's magical and peaceful exit? I don't know what the dragon would have done otherwise, but it's true that Clay had been silently urging the dragon to leave for several moments beforehand. Then again, if dragons

have perfect knowledge of past and future, as some claim, how can a mere mortal affect their actions? Or are there many futures? And if there are, do they branch off in separate directions, never again to touch, or do they all end in the same place, like tributaries of a single river? Perhaps there is even a future that reverses course and travels upriver, as it were? But these are questions for philosophers. Our story has a more modest scope.

The only question we need to answer now is the perennial one. The question every writer faces.

What happens next?

You know how I feel about cruise ships. Nevertheless, I must commend the crew of the *Imperial Conquest*. Captain Abad had spent the last few hours quietly prepping her already well-trained team for the disaster to come. She had an inkling that they would have to evacuate, and she didn't want to overlook a single passenger or crew member. By that measure, she was very successful. She might have lost her ship, but she did not lose any lives.

She even found time to hand out a few treats as she did the rounds of the muster rooms, bidding her passengers good-bye. It was in this way that she ran into Brett Perry's son, the boy who'd been pushed off the ship. There was no time to learn how he'd survived the fall, but she didn't think she'd ever forget how grateful he looked when she handed him the last of the Jell-O parfaits. To think a little bit of sugar and gelatin and whipped cream could make someone so happy!

Unfortunately, there was not enough time for all passengers to get to their assigned muster rooms—some of which were on fire or full of water. Even so, most passengers were safely escorted onto tenders. A few were forced to jump, but they wore life preservers and didn't have to swim far before being picked up.

Later, news reports about the sinking of the *Imperial Conquest* noted the surprising number of farm animals aboard. Sadly, a few of the animals could not be saved, but there were many heartwarming stories about people who had managed to fit chickens and sheep, and in one case even a pig, onto their tenders and taken them to Price Island, where they were released into the wild.

What went unreported—and almost but not quite unnoticed—was the part that sea animals played in the rescue work. Gulls circled the wreck, squawking loudly when they saw a person in danger of drowning or getting caught in the fire. Meanwhile, dolphins, seemingly obeying mysterious commands, picked up stray swimmers as they jumped from the flaming ship.

Only Brett thought to look up—and saw the shimmering shadow of the dragon flying overhead. But even he couldn't see Clay, sitting astride the dragon's neck, speaking the strange words of the Occulta Draco.

It may seem to you that somebody should have stopped Amber and Brett senior from escaping, as they did in a small but fast speedboat that had been stowed discreetly on the cruise ship for precisely this kind of eventuality. But I'm afraid nobody was thinking about them. You have the advantage of seeing the situation from a distance. "What about the villains? Get them!" you say. Our heroes were in the thick of the moment, alas. Now that the dragon was flying free, they were worried only about getting themselves and the people around them safely to shore.

I will report one further tidbit, however, in the hope that it appeases you somewhat. Not many hours later, that same speedboat rendezvoused with a sleek white yacht somewhere in the middle of the Pacific. When Amber climbed aboard, she was immediately slapped across the face by a beautiful blond woman with long white gloves. And Brett senior? He was pushed back into the water by one of the yacht's crew members and forced to swim, angry and humiliated, back to his speedboat.

It is no use, our trying to imagine what it was like for Clay to ride on Ariella's back. The thrill of flying with a dragon is surely like nothing else. But lest you be too jealous of Clay, I have it on good authority that Ariella flew a little higher than Clay would have liked—he apparently got a nosebleed—and that he feared for his life more than once during their flight.

Much worse, of course, was when the dragon landed—very close to the entrance of the dragon cave—and raised its neck so high that Clay had no choice but to slide off. I don't think Clay necessarily expected to spend the night curled up in the cave with Ariella, but he *certainly* didn't expect what happened next: As soon as Clay was safely deposited on the ground, the dragon beat its wings and was aloft again, heading not toward its volcano home but toward the sea.

"So is this, like, good-bye?" Clay asked, unwilling to believe the dragon was really leaving.

Dragons don't say good-bye came the response. But as the great beast flew out over the ocean, it tipped its wing in a way that seemed to mean just that.

Later that evening, when Clay joined his friends on the beach, he noticed a glass bottle by his foot. Inside was a note in his brother's handwriting.

What's better than a knight who slays a dragon?

A knight who saves a dragon.

Clay looked around, hoping briefly that he might see his brother somewhere nearby, but of course he didn't. No doubt Max-Ernest had left in pursuit of Amber and the Midnight Sun.

And yet, despite having been abandoned by the dragon and by his brother as well, Clay felt surprisingly happy. He didn't even mind that it was Flint, risen from the half-dead, who was welcoming him and his friends ashore. He was just glad to be back on this island that was beginning to feel strangely like home.

Besides, he had an overdue library book to return.

EPILOGUE

It is not often that a dragon flies over that great smoggy basin known as Los Angeles. You might think that dragons would feel at home in a place once called the Land of Many Smokes, but to the best of my knowledge, there had been no dragon sightings there for thousands, perhaps millions, of years.

The time was barely five a.m., and the sky was still dark when the great winged serpent appeared on the horizon. It could have been a passenger jet returning from Japan or Hawaii, except for the slow, steady beat of its wings and the occasional swish of its tail.

A few sleepy kids boarding a whale-watching boat in San Pedro were the first to see it. They pointed excitedly, spilling their hot chocolates, but their parents were too absorbed in adult conversation to notice.

Soon others—sailors and dockworkers and truckers and sanitation workers—spotted the great flying beast. They captured fleeting images on their phones and sent them to their friends.

#giantseabird

#mutantflyingfish?

#lookslikeadragon

#theendiscoming

The dragon flew north along the coast, past the surfers of Huntington Beach and the Rollerbladers of the Venice Beach boardwalk. At the Santa Monica Pier, Latin American fishermen missed the first nibbles on their lines because they were staring up at *la gran serpiente*.

At Sunset Boulevard, the dragon turned inland and followed that legendary street as if it were a long winding river that stretched from the ocean through Beverly Hills and beyond.

As the dragon flew over the mansions of the rich and famous, normally reclusive residents stepped outside to catch a glimpse. Drivers gawked from their cars, causing more than one accident. Luckily, it was not yet rush hour. The traffic snarled but did not stop altogether, as it might have.

For its part, the dragon regarded the commotion with something like curiosity—if a beast as ancient and all-knowing as a dragon can be curious—but then seemed to lose interest, as if it had suddenly realized that all those smoke-spewing four-wheeled creatures below were metal, and wouldn't make a very good meal.

The dragon passed more of LA's postcard sites— Mulholland Drive, the Hollywood sign, the Griffith Observatory—without so much as a glance in their direction. But both Dodger Stadium and the Rose Bowl briefly caught the dragon's attention. It circled the stadiums, perhaps mistaking them for volcanic craters or considering their possibilities as nests, and then it flew on.

By now, blurred footage of the flying beast was being uploaded all over the Internet. One picture that caught the dragon in a brown smoggy haze was particularly popular; #smauginthesmog was the most common hashtag.

The city was used to blimps and fireworks and movie-star sightings, but even in LA, a dragon was remarkable. Not since a decommissioned space shuttle had cruised over the city did a flying object command such widespread attention.

Amateur zoologists, special-effects specialists, and conspiracy theorists of all kinds examined every pixel of every picture on Instagram. They measured the dragon's wingspan (just like a raptor!, a ten-year-old commenter noted) and its tail movements (too regular to be made by an animal, said one; too natural to be made by a machine, said another). They even took stock of the dragon's chemical emissions and carbon footprint.

Most people assumed it was a fake, a drone aircraft dressed up as a dragon. Another movie was being filmed, probably. Or else it was a publicity stunt, a clever way to promote a new TV show or video game.

Some people speculated that the citizens of the City of Angels were experiencing a mass collective hallucination. With all the acting and filmmaking and general faking that went on in LA, Angelenos could no longer tell illusion from reality. Their lives had become a fantasy. Or so the logic went.

The people who came closest to the truth were, of course, the youngest children, whose minds were not closed to the possibility of a dragon. And the ranchers outside the city, whose livestock were soon lost to the dragon's claws. They couldn't afford not to believe.

In a matter of days, the dragon was largely forgotten. On to the next news cycle.

You see, when something exciting and inexplicable happens, the world wants to know about it; but if it remains unexplained for too long, the world turns away. We don't want to know that there are things we don't understand.

However, a few select and secretive groups of people around the globe—some of whom you have met in this narrative, others whom you may yet meet in another—knew exactly what they were seeing when they looked at pictures of the dragon on their newsfeeds. They knew the dragon was real, and they knew where the dragon had come from, if not where the dragon was going.

Some of these people rejoiced that the dragon was free; others were angry that it had escaped their grasp.

The bad guys had not won. But neither, it must be said, had the good guys. Not yet.

For the moment, at least, the dragon had won. And a dragon is neither good nor bad. It just is.

BACK MATTER*

MAGICA *AND* SCIENTIA: *A MYTH*

Long ago, when the earth had just learned to talk and the moon was still in diapers, a pair of twins was born. Magic and Science were their names—or

---

* *BACK MATTER* IS WHAT PUBLISHERS CALL ALL THE STUFF IN A BOOK THAT COMES AFTER THE LAST PAGE OF A STORY, SUCH AS AN APPENDIX OR AN ACKNOWLEDGMENTS SECTION. AS MY READERS KNOW, I USUALLY INCLUDE AN APPENDIX AT THE END OF MY BOOKS. (I NEVER HAVE ACKNOWLEDGMENTS BECAUSE THAT WOULD MEAN ACKNOWLEDGING THAT THERE ARE PEOPLE OTHER THAN MYSELF WHO HELP CREATE MY BOOKS, AND I WOULD NEVER ACKNOWLEDGE THAT!) AT THE SAME TIME, I'VE ALWAYS BEEN UNCOMFORTABLE USING THE TERM *APPENDIX* BECAUSE IT SOUNDS SO SERIOUS AND INFORMATIONAL; IT IMPLIES THAT THE READER MIGHT LEARN SOMETHING—A DUBIOUS PROPOSITION AT BEST. FOR THIS BOOK, I CHOSE THE TERM *BACK MATTER* INSTEAD BECAUSE IT REMINDS ME OF *DARK MATTER*—WHICH, AS YOU MAY KNOW, IS WHAT ASTROPHYSICISTS CALL THE MYSTERIOUS STUFF THAT MOST OF THE UNIVERSE HAPPENS TO BE MADE OF. NEITHER EMITTING NOR ABSORBING LIGHT, DARK MATTER HAS NEVER BEEN SEEN BY HUMAN EYES. ITS EXISTENCE IS PURE SPECULATION. WE KNOW NOTHING ABOUT IT, AND YET WE'D BE NOTHING WITHOUT IT. NOW, *THAT* IS THE SORT OF "INFORMATION" I CAN GET BEHIND. IF I CAN FIND IT.

Magica and *Scientia*, if you like your myths to sound mythological.

Magic and Science were smart, lively children, a girl and a boy respectively, and they loved each other very much.

Together they wondered at rainbows, studied the stars, and sailed the oceans; they concocted powerful potions and conducted explosive experiments; and they cavorted with all manner of creatures, many of which we no longer have names for, and most of which we would be very surprised to see roaming the world today.

When something happened that they didn't understand, Magic and Science made up stories about it. When the earth shook or the skies stormed or a volcano erupted or they got pimples on their noses, they blamed the event on warring gods or raging monsters, or simply on the movement of the celestial spheres.*

These stories weren't right or wrong; they were just stories. They were ways for Magic and Science to

---

* IN THE ANCIENT WORLD, SCHOLARS BELIEVED THAT THE STARS WERE EMBEDDED IN INVISIBLE SPHERES—MADE OF A FANTASTICAL FIFTH ELEMENT CALLED THE QUINTESSENCE—THAT ROTATED AROUND THE EARTH, LIKE GIANT JEWEL-ENCRUSTED BUBBLES. NOWADAYS, OF COURSE, WE KNOW OUR UNIVERSE TO BE RULED BY ANOTHER SORT OF CELESTIAL SPHERE ALTOGETHER—THE SORT THAT SURROUNDS A CELEBRITY LIKE A POP SINGER OR YOUTUBE STAR.

describe their world and their lives and their noses and other things that appeared in front of their faces.

But as they grew older, the siblings started to drift apart.

Magic was always showing off. Look at me, look at me, she would say. I can predict the future, I can make gold, I can live forever. Who needs boring old Science when you can have fantastic, fabulous, magical me?

Magic's proclamations didn't have much of a factual basis, and sometimes they were downright deceptive, but she was beautiful and fun, and her hair was always changing color, and for a long time she was more popular than Science.

Being only human, Science grew jealous.

One by one, Science started taking things away from Magic.

Look, said Magic. I can make a fire by rubbing two sticks together. They are my magic wands.

That's called combustion, said Science. He stomped out the fire.

Well, watch this—I can make this apple move by itself, joked Magic. She let go of the apple, and it dropped to the ground. See, she said, and laughed.

That's just gravity, said Science, not laughing. He picked up the apple and ate it.

Well, have you seen me light the night sky like Zeus himself? Surely that is magic, said Magic.

Lightning is electricity. It is science, said Science. And you'd better be careful or lightning might strike your umbrella and fry your precious hair—not that it isn't already ruined by all that bleaching.

Science kept taking things for himself until even the stars themselves were his; no longer glittering jewels embedded in mysterious invisible spheres, they were just balls of gas floating in a void.

Once joyous and carefree, Magic turned cranky and careworn. You win, she said to her brother. Take everything. Just leave me alone. Rarely did she go out in public, and when she did, she wore tinfoil hats and walked her cat on a leash. She had been everyone's favorite; now people called her a witch, a hag, a harridan.

Ha! I told you so, said Science. Magic is nothing. I, Science, am everything.

By now, Science was very strong and powerful; and, it must be admitted, he solved many of the world's ills with his wide knowledge and his brilliant discoveries. Alas, he was not satisfied. For always there was something new that he did not understand. And when there was nothing new, there was still something very old, something that plagued him all his life; and his life was very long because although he was human, he was also a mythological figure, and mythological figures take a long time to die.

Almost as long as dragons take to die, and dragons were the very old thing that plagued him all his life.

No matter how hard he tried, Science could not explain dragons. They breathed fire, yet they had no internal combustion engines. They flew as if they were weightless, and yet their scales were as heavy as lead. Worst of all, they smiled their terrible smiles, and Science never got the joke. He wasn't even sure there was a joke.

You see, dragons are unknowable because they *are* the unknown. This may sound redundant, or like a tautology, if you know what a tautology is, but that's only because you're not a dragon.* At the same time, even though they are the unknown, dragons know all. Dragons are the wildest beasts in the world, but they are also the wisest. This may sound contradictory, or like a paradox, if you know what a paradox is, but again that's only because you're not a dragon.**

Unless you are a dragon. Which would very much surprise me. It would also scare me. I hope you're not a dragon.

Back to the myth:

Magic was not scared of dragons. She thought dragons were cute. At least, she thought they were

---

* A TAUTOLOGY IS A STATEMENT OR IDEA THAT REPEATS ITSELF IN ORDER TO PROVE ITS TRUTH, WHICH IS WHY A STATEMENT OR IDEA THAT REPEATS ITSELF IN ORDER TO PROVE ITS TRUTH IS A TAUTOLOGY.

** A PARADOX IS A STATEMENT OR IDEA THAT SEEMS TO CONTRADICT ITSELF BUT THAT MIGHT NONETHELESS BE TRUE. IF, FOR EXAMPLE, YOU WERE TO GAIN KNOWLEDGE FROM FOOTNOTES AS FOOLISH AND MISLEADING AS MINE, THAT WOULD BE QUITE PARADOXICAL.

cute when she was a young girl and she was lucky enough to see some baby dragons hatching from their shells. (*Awww.*) She had seen few dragons in the years since and now had no particular opinion about whether they were cute or not, but if pressed, she probably would have said not. When you are scorned by everyone you meet, you don't find many things cute.

In any event, when a very old and very large dragon unexpectedly alighted on the doorstep of her cave, its long dragon tail knocking over her favorite yew tree and its fiery dragon breath singeing her cat's fur, her first thought was not that the dragon was cute. Her first thought was that the dragon had better have a very good reason for visiting, and that is exactly what she told the dragon.

We are here because you called us, said the dragon. Although the dragon didn't exactly say it. (As you may know, dragons don't really *say* anything. If they want to communicate an idea to you, the idea just appears in your head as if it's always been there. It's a bit like being hypnotized. It can be disconcerting if you're not used to it.)

I don't remember calling you, said Magic.

You will, said the dragon.

I will call you, or I will remember calling you?

A distinction without a difference, said the dragon. It is time to go.

Where are we going? asked Magic.

Humans never know where they are going; that is their curse. Dragons always do; that is ours.

Magic knew enough about dragons to know that when a dragon offers you a ride, you don't say no. She climbed up onto the dragon's back, taking only her hat and her umbrella.

Wait! cried Magic as the dragon took off with a great flapping of wings. We forgot my cat!

Did we? said the dragon ambiguously.

With its great dragon claws, the dragon scooped up the cat; and with its great dragon jaws, the dragon bit down on the cat. As Magic shrieked in surprise, the dragon flew away with her on its back, and one of those infuriating dragon smiles on its lips.

WHAT IS THE MORAL OF THE STORY?

a) Never mind elephants; it's dragons that never forget.

b) Dragons don't like cats, except as snacks.

c) Science was right about one thing: Dragons have a terrible sense of humor.

d) Only when dragons return will magic be restored to our world.

e) All of the above.